'Good morning, Lucy! You choose very early hours for your morning calls, don't you?'

Startled, she stumbled to her feet. 'JJ!'

He gave her one of his half-smiles. 'What were you trying to do, make sure the old boy won't sell his land to me?'

She blushed a fiery red. 'And if I was, are you surprised? After your rudeness yesterday I'd do anything to make you give up this deal!' she answered passionately.

'I really get up your nose, don't I?' he answered. 'You should be old enough not to resent the truth when you hear it!'

INDEPENDENT LADY

BY
KRISTY McCALLUM

MILLS & BOON LIMITED
ETON HOUSE   18-24 PARADISE ROAD
RICHMOND   SURREY   TW9 1SR

*First published in Great Britain 1988
by Mills & Boon Limited*

© Kristy McCallum 1988

*Australian copyright 1988
Philippine copyright 1989
This edition 1989*

ISBN 0 263 76226 2

*Set in Times Roman 11 on 12½ pt.
01-8902-44709 C*

Made and printed in Great Britain

CHAPTER ONE

'OH, darling! Why on earth do you want to go and live there?'

Lucy looked quickly up at her mother, then sighed. 'I thought I had just explained why, and...' she shook her head ruefully, 'I hoped you would understand.'

'The whole idea is crazy!' Mrs Porter sat up straighter in her chair. 'I quite realise that you're finding it difficult to do your work in London, but why not come home? We'd love to have you here, wouldn't we, darling?' she appealed to her husband.

Cool, grey eyes similar to his daughter's crinkled with sudden amusement as he took in Lucy's appalled expression. 'I think our daughter is old enough now to decide what's best for her...' He ignored his wife's disappointment and smiled openly at Lucy, who grinned back at him. 'I take it that you have thought this whole idea out carefully?'

'Of course I have, Daddy! There's nothing to keep me in London, and you must remember how happy I always was with Aunt Mary.'

Her father looked at her carefully, steepling his fingers as he always did when considering a problem. A lifetime as a country solicitor had taught him to consider his words meticulously. 'It won't be the same, you know. Sometimes it's a mistake to go back in time and expect to find everything just the same...'

Lucy hunched a slightly pettish shoulder. 'I know that! I'm not a child any more.'

She gave her mother a dark look, and John Porter hurriedly intervened before his wife could interrupt further. 'You realise that French inheritance laws are different from ours, don't you?' Lucy gave him a slightly blank look. 'When a property is left jointly, then it is always divided into equal halves between the legatees.'

'But that isn't the case, is it?' she reminded him quickly. 'Aunt Mary always intended that Cherrytree Farm would be mine one day, whatever happened!'

'Yes, that's so. I drew up the deeds myself with Gilbert's lawyers at the time of their marriage, but I do slightly wonder if Jean-Louis realises that is the case.'

Lucy looked her astonishment. 'Why should you think that will bother him? Grande Ferme is nearly three times as big as Cherrytree, so why should my little inheritance concern him?'

John Porter didn't smile this time at Lucy's indignation. 'Because the only access to the beach is through Cherrytree,' he told her, 'and...'

'That won't worry Jean-Louis!' Lucy interrupted, not waiting for her father to finish. 'I can't see him settling down happily to a life on the farm. Why, he's a Parisian born and bred, and he'll sell the farm as quickly as possible!'

Her father looked as if he was on the point of continuing to speak, but stopped himself as his wife interrupted impetuously.

'Really, John! You have to agree that Lucy is perfectly right. Why, I even remember him telling me when he was quite young...' She launched into a story to prove her point, and John Porter found himself facing two pairs of accusing eyes at the end of it.

He held out a hand, then laughed ruefully. 'I don't deny that you are both right, my darlings, but I'm still not entirely convinced that Jean-Louis realises exactly how things are left. If, for instance, there was to be any question of development, then Cherrytree would be vital to his plans.'

'Development? Oh, no, I couldn't bear it!' Lucy got up and walked over to her father, her arms tightly folded over her chest. 'Why are you saying this? Have you heard from him?'

'No, I've heard nothing, but it isn't beyond the bounds of possibility to guess that he will try to get the best price he can for it.'

Lucy gave a great sigh of relief. 'I can't see him bothering. He will be too tied up with his job in Paris and with Pascale. Anyway, both Gilbert and

Aunt Mary would have hated the idea, he knows that as well as I do!'

Her father gave her a slightly worried look. 'It isn't a particularly French characteristic to allow oneself to be bothered by sentiment if there is a considerable amount of money involved!'

Lucy shrugged her shoulders. 'I should have thought Jean-Louis' family was quite well off enough not to have to bother to go to those lengths over the sale of an unwanted farm!' she answered scornfully. 'Anyway, whatever his plans, he won't be able to do anything, because I shall certainly refuse to sell!'

John Porter stood up and reached for his pipe, which was on the mantelpiece. When he had got it going satisfactorily he looked at his daughter's slightly flushed face with a rueful expression in his own. 'I see you have made up your mind, and nothing's going to stop you going there, is it?' He smiled slightly. 'Oh, well! If you run into any problems you can always call on me. Later on, in summer, your mother and I will come and visit you, when you've had time to get yourself sorted out!'

Lucy ran over to give him a hug. 'Thank you, Daddy! Although at the age of twenty-five I think I'm quite capable of sorting out any problems on my own!'

'You're so independent, darling...' Her mother gave a sigh. 'At your age I was already married, and here you are, rushing off to France to be by yourself. I must say I don't understand you...'

Her daughter grinned at her, relaxed now she had her father's agreement to do what she wanted. 'Never mind—who knows, I might meet a dashing Frenchman who'll sweep me off my feet!'

Mrs Porter gave her a faintly malicious smile. 'It would do you a power of good, my dear, to meet some man who isn't going to be bowled over by your looks! You've had your own way for too long, and it isn't good for you!' On this valedictory note she left the room, ignoring the surprised looks on her husband's and daughter's faces.

'Well!' Lucy interjected. 'She is upset, isn't she?'

'I think you'll find that she's just a frustrated grandmother at the moment! Angela Pope was here yesterday telling her all about her newest grandaughter!'

'Oh, dear! Poor Mummy, perhaps it's a good thing I'm going away...'

Her father gave her a quick look. 'Don't you start to worry! You'll meet the right man some day, although I hope you won't take as long as Aunt Mary to do it!'

'I suppose so, but at the risk of upsetting Mummy further I have to confess that I intend to be far too busy for the next few months to bother to look!'

Her father laughed. 'Well, as long you're happy I'm not complaining. I like to have my only child around.'

*   *   *

Lucy handed over her ticket to the bored-looking attendant at Newhaven who was checking the small queue of cars waiting to catch the early-morning ferry to Dieppe. As it had been cold when she'd left home she had crammed her long, blonde hair into a woollen cap. Her pale suede jacket was zipped up to the neck and she was grateful for the warmth of her fawn cords. There seemed to be no hurry, so she switched off the engine of her car and got out to lean against it, one hand masking a yawn. The fresh, salty air was being blown in from the sea, and idly she looked around at her fellow passengers.

They were mostly lorry drivers, it was too early in the year to attract many tourists, and Lucy's car was for the moment the last in line of the twenty or so ahead of her. She blinked sleepily and half smiled at a couple of lorry drivers whose piercing wolf-whistles had attracted her attention. She was used to more than her share of male attention, but even so it was gratifying to get it at a quarter to seven on a cold grey morning of spring when she was muffled up like a bear in winter clothes.

The cars ahead started to move forward slowly, so without checking behind her she got back into her car. The Ford Escort Cabriolet was her pride and joy. She loved driving fast, priding herself on her expertise, and she had ignored her parents' protests when she had blown all her grandmother's legacy on buying herself the fastest and sportiest car she could afford.

She loved the attention she got from other drivers—at the slightest opportunity she drove with the hood down, her long hair streaming out behind her, revelling in the sensation of speed the drophead gave her. If the weather in France was as good as she had heard, then it was going to be heaven to drive around with the hood down after the late spring they had had at home.

She moved forward confidently towards the bowels of the ship, over the metal ramps and towards the organised chaos ahead. She had quite deliberately left a long gap between herself and the car in front, disliking the starting and stopping every few yards, and she accelerated smoothly under the imperious demands of one of the crew organising the cars and lorries packed tightly, nose to tail. She advanced steadily, stopping abruptly as his arm flashed down in front of her, and felt a bump from behind. Her car lurched forward under the impact and she heard a tinkle of glass as one of the lights caught on the bumper of the car ahead of her.

Furious, she put on the handbrake and got out to inspect the damage, then turned to glare at the driver who had caused the trouble. She had an impression of vital good looks. Blue eyes, heavily lidded, that looked as if they would habitually crinkle into warm laughter, straight brows and brown hair, worn slightly long. The mouth was full, wide and beautifully curved, although at the moment the face expressed nothing but boredom and irritation at what had happened. It was impossible to deny that he was an exceptionally attractive man.

He was wearing faded blue jeans and a designer knitted sweater over a plain white shirt, but his eyes slid over her with unflattering speed as if she was worthy of no special attention. Her eyes widened as she took in his car; it was a Ferrari, but not the vivid red that was their trademark. This was painted black, and was sleek and powerful, its subdued colour quite unable to disguise its predatory lines. Irrationally, that fanned the flames of her temper. Here was a man who appeared on the surface to have everything, including a car she had dreamed of driving ever since she had first passed her driving test. Her chest swelled with indignation as, ignoring her, he walked past to check the Escort's damage with the crew member. The glass from one of her headlights had been smashed, and between them they were carefully collecting the long, dangerous shards of glass.

'Why on earth couldn't you have been more careful?'

Blue eyes, now cold, looked up and surveyed her sardonically. 'Your sudden stop caught me unawares. I'm sorry.'

'Sorry! I should hope you are, but what about my car?'

'Don't worry, miss.' She had forgotten the sailor, and turned towards him, just catching the tail end of a grin he had given the man. 'It's only the glass that has been broken, nothing serious,' he added soothingly.

'All the same,' cold blue eyes regarded her indifferently, 'you'd better check the bulb works.'

She turned back to the owner of the Ferrari, made even crosser by his air of scarcely concealed irritation, but did as he suggested, to find the light seemed to work perfectly. 'I'm not driving all over France with a broken headlight, it'll have to be mended!'

'We can't do it aboard the ferry, miss, you'll have to wait until you find a garage. You can claim off your insurance.' The sailor's conciliating grin enraged her even further.

'I'm not claiming off my insurance! It wasn't my fault.' By now she had decided that the stranger's good looks masked a distinctly unattractive personality, and there was a belligerent look on her face as she turned back to him. 'What's your name?'

His eyes held her furious grey ones as, without looking, he dropped the pieces of glass he had collected into a bucket the sailor silently offered him. His face tightened, and she got the uncomfortable impression that he was somehow amused by her anger, but before she had a chance to explode into speech he answered her. 'I don't think it will be necessary to bother any insurance company over such a minor affair.' His eyes continued to hold hers as he put his hand in his pocket and drew out a notecase. He extracted several large notes of French francs and handed them over to her. 'This should be more than enough to replace the glass and cover any garage charges that may occur.'

She looked at the notes held out to her, indecision written all over her face.

'That's very generous, miss; I should accept if I were you . . .'

She gave the crewman a resentful look, well aware that his sympathies did not lie with her. 'All right, well, thank you . . .' she took the notes from him ' . . . but you've given me much too much. Where shall I send the change?'

One corner of his mouth lifted in a half-smile. 'Forget it! Keep it as compensation for the annoyance.' Before she was given a chance to refuse curtly, he moved elegantly away to the stairs, leaving her with her mouth open at the insolent ease with which he thought money solved the problem.

'Well!' she said, aware that she had allowed herself to be out-manoeuvred by his offer.

'Very generous of the gentleman,' the sailor added obsequiously, also looking after the tall figure until he disappeared from sight. 'It shouldn't cost you more than a quarter of that to put the damage right.' Feeling that the matter had been satisfactorily settled, he walked away to continue his job, leaving Lucy behind, biting her lip in frustration until she too decided to make her way up the stairs to the decks above.

The stranger had definitely been insulting in the way he had offered her money, as if that would quell all argument, and she intended to find him and return most of it immediately. She wondered who he was; those arrogant good looks had obviously made sure that he was not unaware of his impact on her sex. She felt a mounting determination to let him know that she didn't intend to be brushed aside as if she was of no more importance than a fly that had bothered him. He might be used to women falling at his feet, but she intended to make it clear that as far as she was concerned he left her cold. Her ready sense of humour asserted itself as she thought of their coming meeting. Shock had momentarily deprived her of her usual self-possession, but Mr Ferrari was going to be in for a surprise when she caught up with him. She would have great pleasure in returning to him nearly all his money, less the small amount she thought it would cost to replace the glass.

Half an hour later she owned herself beaten. He seemed to have totally disappeared, and she had missed watching the ferry depart. He had to be either on the bridge with the captain or in the crew's quarters somewhere, because she was sure she had covered every other part of the ferry. She went down to the canteen and ordered herself a coffee and a roll; the drama combined with the sea air had given her an appetite. As she slowly sipped her coffee, common sense reasserted itself. She would see him when they docked at Dieppe; there was no way he could get off the ferry before her. She finished her coffee in a happier frame of mind, and moved back outside to watch the coast of England slowly receding as the ferry ploughed its way through the slightly choppy sea. She was pleased she was a good sailor because, although the sea could not be described as rough, it seemed as unsettled as the weather she hoped she would soon be leaving behind.

The cold wind made it necessary for her to walk to keep warm, but as she explored the ship her thoughts, which should have been all for her plans in the days ahead, were mysteriously mixed up with the good-looking, arrogant stranger who had entered her life so dramatically. It was rare to meet any man who appeared indifferent to her particular brand of golden good looks. It wasn't that she was particularly vain, she told herself, it was just, well, unusual to get such a negative response from a member of the opposite sex.

An only child, she had learnt early in her life that she could twist her father around her little finger. Because she had a warm, happy personality she had never had the slightest difficulty in attracting people to her. Her mother had confidently expected an early marriage, but here she was, twenty-five years old and no nearer than she had ever been to fulfilling her mother's hopes for her. For all her apparently easy-going personality, there was a stubborn streak buried inside her which would never let her settle for second best. None of the many men she had been out with had ever managed to touch her heart seriously for any length of time. As she grew older she had come to despise their easy capitulation to her looks, and, although she wasn't quite at the despairing age, she now tended to channel most of her energies into her work.

She was no fool, and knew that her girlfriends envied her her power to catch most men's eyes, but just lately it had become an empty victory. They had become so boringly predictable in what they wanted from her. She smiled to herself; if she was to be honest, it was the stranger's apparent indifference to her looks that had caught her interest. He might have infuriated her, but she would enjoy trying to put him in his place when they met again.

She leant over the rail, ignoring the wind which blew stray tendrils of hair loose from its woolly confines as the ferry passed the outer wall of Dieppe harbour. Already the sun was warming her face, and she was soon joined by other passengers as the ship moved forward smoothly to its appointed mooring. The tannoy, voice blaring, asking for drivers to return to their cars, caught her unawares.

Startled, she dropped her shoulder bag and watched with dismay her car keys slip out of it and down a small grating near the edge of the deck. She bent down hurriedly, trying to retrieve them, but she couldn't move the grating; she could just see them, glinting softly beneath her probing fingers.

'You'll have to get help, my dear.' A middle-aged lady and her husband rose unsteadily off their knees. 'I'm sorry, but you are going to need one of the crew, I'm afraid.' Lucy thanked them as they left to return to their own car. Easier said than done, she told herself grimly a quarter of an hour later as the deck emptied except for the day-trippers, and the only crew she could see were busy with ropes and far too occupied to acknowledge her. With a rising sense of panic she ran back inside the ship, but all the bars and restaurants were now closed, with no sign of the stewards. Defeated, she came out again, wondering whether to brave the roped-off section that led up to the bridge. The ferry had been tied up some time before she was able to get help from a young crewman. It didn't take him long to get her keys, but by now the first cars were already driving off the ship.

Furious at her clumsiness, she raced down to the lower deck to find that all the cars in front and the one behind hers had already left. She was greeted with weary resignation by the crew member who had helped her before. 'More trouble, miss?' He took in her breathless state and the disappointment in her eyes, and raised his own in disbelief as she gasped out the story of the missing keys. Understandably, he seemed keen to get her off the ferry before anything else happened to her, and she could almost hear his unspoken comment about women drivers. Her hand shook slightly with indignation as she turned on the ignition, but she managed to leave with no more damage to the car or her dignity.

The traffic near Rouen slowed her down, and as it was already so much warmer she was longing to find a garage and change her clothes for something cooler. She turned into the Avenue de Paris, hoping it was not too far from the main square, with relief. The garage there carried the spares that were needed and she was soon in friendly negotiation. They even offered her a small room where she could safely change her clothes, and, ignoring the pin-ups on the walls, she quickly put on a blouse and skirt and some open sandals, tidying herself in a cracked piece of mirror. They were going to keep her car while she explored the town and had lunch before continuing on her way.

She was handed a card with the name of the garage on it and struck out for the main square and the cathedral, the sun warming her arms and legs. She was acutely conscious of her winter paleness and hoped that the soft grey and white stripes of her outfit didn't make her appear as pale as a ghost.

Later, as she stood under the chiselled cliff of the west front of the great building that soared towards

the blue sky her thoughts were far from herself.
The splendour and beauty of the cathedral possessed all her senses. Still bemused, she moved
slowly towards a *brasserie* to order lunch. A small,
clipped hedge of box, so beloved of the French,
planted in red containers, marked a corner of the
square. Red and white checked paper tablecloths
added to the attraction, and with a small sigh of
satisfaction she sat down at one of the few empty
tables left. The animated chatter around her, the
delicious smell of freshly ground coffee, all gave
her a feeling of intense happiness. A small grey
poodle, in a collar and lead of pure scarlet, was
begging for sugar lumps from its mistress, its ridiculous little pompom of a tail helping it to keep
its balance. Its owner, a supremely smart woman
of middle age, was in animated conversation with
her companion, but Lucy noted with amusement
that she was dipping sugar lumps into her coffee
and, without looking, feeding them to the dog.

She thought this place was the very essence of
France, as if it had distilled itself into this tiny
fragment of time purely for her own pleasure. The
smells, the noise, and above all the wonderful gothic
building that towered above the square, its outline
endlessly obscured by the scattered clouds of
pigeons that wheeled in front of it. She committed
the scene to memory and ordered a glass of white
wine as she studied the menu, trying to decide what
she most wanted to eat.

'Lucy! This is a wonderful surprise!'

She looked up into the dark brown eyes gazing soulfully into her own. 'Jean-Louis! What on earth are you doing here?'

'I'm on my way to Grande Ferme, of course! This is fantastic luck to meet like this. May I join you?' She smiled her agreement and watched with amusement as he carefully looked at the chair before sitting down on it. He was just as immaculately turned out as he used to be as a child when they shared holidays on La Ferme Cerisier.

'I tried to call you at home to see if you could come and meet me at the farm, and when your mother told me you were on your way I decided to leave at once. It will be like the old days, won't it? A journey into the past, and all the fun we used to have when we were children.' He gave her one of his old, admiring looks. 'It's been too long since we have met, Lucy. You get more beautiful every year! Tante Elizabeth tells me there is still no one special in your life, but I find that very hard to believe...' He picked up one of her hands and kissed the back of it.

Lucy laughed with real pleasure. 'You haven't changed a bit, Jean-Louis! Anyway, what about Pascale?'

He waved one arm carelessly as if she was of no importance. 'Pascale! We are a little bored of each other at the moment. She has been in England working for JJ O'Donnell. She told me it was to

improve her English but, as she has only just returned after six months, I think there is a little more
to it than that!'

Lucy wasn't fooled by his careless words. 'I'm
sorry, I shouldn't have asked,' she answered in
quick sympathy.

'But yes, why not? She is still my fiancée, you
know.' His eyes teased her warmly. 'Of course, if
you had agreed to marry me all those years ago
when I first asked you, then Pascale and I would
never have got together!'

'Liar! You've always adored her. I knew that even
when we were all children together!'

He shrugged his shoulders expressively. 'Maybe,
once, but now it is different; perhaps we made a
mistake.'

'No, you didn't!' she replied warmly. 'I've always
thought you were both perfect for each other.'

They were both quiet for a moment, reliving the
past. Ever since Jean-Louis' uncle, Gilbert DuParc,
had married Lucy's aunt Mary, they had spent their
summers together at her aunt's smaller farm on the
coast. Jean-Louis had been fourteen when they first
met, Lucy two years younger. Pascale was the only
daughter of Jean-Louis' parents' friends in Paris.
The same age as Lucy, she too had spent part of
her summers at the farm. Small and neat, with a
warm olive skin and a very pretty face, she had
always protested that the farms were no fun for a
holiday, even though they were within walking dis-

tance of the beach. She had always preferred the more sophisticated pleasures of life and yearned for the South of France. She was the only girl Lucy had met who had ever made her feel a little inadequate. She had always been so much more grown-up, and she had made it clear that she found Lucy rather stupid.

Over the years, as Lucy became more beautiful and striking-looking with her long, blonde hair, Pascale made her jealousy clear. She had clung to Jean-Louis like a limpet whenever the three of them were together, making it clear to the English girl that she considered him to be her property.

The last summer they had spent at the farm Lucy had been eighteen, and that year Jean-Louis had dropped all pretence of regarding her as a sister and had concentrated his considerable charm on her. Pascale and her parents hadn't arrived until much later in the summer than usual, so the two of them, apart from their parents, had had nearly three weeks together. They had explored the coast thoroughly on his motorbike and in the evenings had gone out together with their friends to the discos in the neighbouring towns.

That had been the summer he had asked her to marry him, the night before Pascale arrived. Lucy had refused his offer regretfully. She liked him enormously, but he had become too much like a brother in her mind. She knew also that his parents wanted him to marry Pascale eventually, and anyway, they had both been too young to settle down. The French girl's jealousy had made the rest of the summer so uncomfortable that Lucy had decided it would be better if she and her family went somewhere else for their holidays another year. She would be able to see her aunt when she came over to stay with her family, which she did once every year, but all the same she felt sad that she had allowed Pascale to drive her away from her holiday home. She had met Jean-Louis intermittently over the years when he had come to London, but they never again managed to have the easy relationship of their childhood. Lucy had not been very surprised when they had notice of their engagement two years ago, but she had been perturbed that no immediate wedding had been planned.

She found she was curious to find out about Pascale. 'Who is JJ O'Donnell?'

Jean-Louis looked rather shocked at her ignorance. 'Surely you've heard of him, Lucy! He is the man who has made his name developing holiday complexes around Europe.' He looked at her steadily for a moment before dropping his eyes to his hands. 'I understand he could be interested in the farms...'

'Oh, no! You don't really want to see them developed, do you?'

Jean-Louis shifted rather uncomfortably in his chair. 'But what else are we to do with them, Lucy? I live in Paris, you London... We will have to sell.

The whole coast has changed so much since you were last here, even the Brocarts' farm has now been turned into an hotel...'

It was Lucy's turn to wriggle uncomfortably as she remembered her father's words. 'But I don't want to sell! I want to live in Aunt Mary's little house and just keep the old cherry orchard.'

He looked at her with amazement. 'But what do you want to keep it for? I thought your work was in London.'

'I can do my work anywhere, and I'm fed up with London at the moment. I want to try and live here for a change.'

He looked totally unbelieving. 'You want to come and live by yourself in Normandy? You must be mad!'

She sighed; his reaction didn't surprise her—everyone, including her own family, thought she was mad. But there was a restlessness inside her just lately, and not even the success of her work could make her completely happy in London. She knew she needed a change, some space to think things out, and when she'd heard that her aunt had left her her old home she had jumped at the chance of making a different life for herself. Since her gently amusing children's books had sold so successfully at home and in the States, she had a measure of independence to show for all the lean years in the past.

'I don't think I'm mad at all! Believe me, the idea that it will be possible to live at Cherrytree seems like a gift from heaven!'

'But why, Lucy? I don't understand how a girl like you can think of burying herself away here. Has something gone wrong in London? Is it some man who has let you down?'

She tried to ignore the irritation she felt. 'Why do you think I must have had an unhappy love affair? I haven't found any man yet who was worth losing sleep over!' She looked up into the dark brown eyes watching her and saw the expression of bewilderment on his face. She took a deep breath. 'Look, I'll try to explain. For years most of the men who have taken me out don't take my work seriously. Oh, they think I'm quite clever when they read the books, but they are always faintly patronising about them. They seem to expect me to be a beautiful dumb blonde, only interested in clothes and going to bed with them. None of them seems to understand that I take my work seriously, they treat it as an amusing hobby. They expect me to drop everything when they want to take me out and give me a so-called good time. Maybe I've been mixing with the wrong people, but I've been so bored! I'm twenty-five years old and I want to escape and live my own life for a bit! The only people who know me here knew me as a child and they won't bother me! I'll be able to get on with my writing and illustrating in peace and quiet without getting endlessly interrupted. I've been commissioned to do another, slightly longer book and I want it to be a success. My work has been getting a bit stale just lately...' She sighed. 'I was always so happy here, don't you remember?'

'Yes, yes, I do...' His face softened. 'I do understand, Lucy, you need a break. You stay at the farm all summer, and at the end of the season you'll feel a new person! Then we can talk about selling it all.'

She answered him sharply. 'What do you mean, selling it all? I thought you understood. I don't want to sell Aunt Mary's house, I want to keep it and live there all the year round!'

His mouth thinned to a firm line as he saw the determination on her face. 'Look, this isn't the time to discuss it. Let's wait until you get there. You might well change your mind when you see all the changes that have taken place.'

It was difficult to resist Jean-Louis' practised smile; he had always had a great deal of charm when he chose to exert it. He had grown into a good-looking man. As a child he had been almost painfully thin, but his body had now filled out. She thought he was the type of man who would always be elegant, like his uncle Gilbert, and she had to admit that now he looked very fit. She gave him an admiring grin.

'Are you still playing a lot of tennis?'

'Yes, I try to keep in good shape, although it's not so easy now I'm tied to a desk all day.'

'How long can you stay away from the office this time?'

'Only a week, I'm afraid. You won't mind staying at Cherrytree alone?'

'Old Marie is still there, isn't she?' He nodded. 'Well, she'll take care of me, she's expecting me.'

'You're going straight there tonight?'

'No, I'm staying in Caen for a change, I've never been there.'

He looked disappointed for a moment. 'I would offer to come with you, but I've promised Pierre that I'll be arriving this evening so I'd better stick to my plans. He's getting old now and wants to retire, but he's still running everything until he knows our plans. So, until tomorrow, then?'

'Tomorrow,' she echoed with another smile. By common consent they talked no more about their inheritance before parting after lunch, to meet again the next day at Cherrytree Farm.

CHAPTER TWO

LUCY was worried as she left Rouen. Her car was as good as new, but Jean-Louis' hints about developing the farms bothered her. She knew it wouldn't be possible unless she agreed to sell her house, and that was the last thing she intended to do. Cherrytree Farm was more of a smallholding rather than a viable agricultural unit on its own. After he had married her aunt, Gilbert DuParc had run both places together, but Lucy knew that the little farm's chief asset was that it was so near the sea and could be used as a very attractive holiday home. It would certainly earn more money that way than it would ever have done as a farm.

Another reason she was so keen to keep it was because it was from her aunt that she had inherited her ability to draw, and she had always felt a special rapport with her because of it. It had been Aunt Mary who had encouraged her first attempts at drawing all the animals on the farm, and it had been she who had suggested that she should write stories to go with the drawings. She had inherited her dry sense of humour from her solicitor father, but it had always been her aunt who had encouraged her to believe that she could make a career from her skills.

Although her small paperback books were aimed at children, grown-ups liked them and found them amusing as well. Lucy was still amazed at their success, which seemed to grow every year, and she was under pressure from her publishers to produce more and more books to keep up with the demand. It was this pressure that had prompted her to leave London and really concentrate on her work, and, as she had had her first inspiration at Cherrytree Farm, then this was where she wanted to return. Her aunt's death, sad though it was, had seemed almost providential when she had heard that she was to be the new owner of the one place where she knew she would be able to work undisturbed.

She drove into Caen slowly and parked the car near the centre of the town before starting to explore, but as she walked round the Abbaye des Dames and the Abbaye des Hommes she found herself unable to really appreciate their beauty. It was Jean-Louis and his possible plans that obsessed her, and she found she couldn't really concentrate on the sights around her. Maybe her mood was wrong, she thought, but to her Caen lacked the charm of Bayeux, even if it was one of the most prosperous towns in Normandy.

The evening air was definitely cool as she finished her sightseeing and went to find her car. Reluctantly she put the roof up before driving off to

find the discreet and expensive hotel where she was
staying the night as a sop to her mother's worries
about sleeping alone in France.

She drove carefully through the busy streets full
of people going home after a day's work, and admitted to herself that she felt unusually tired and
depressed. All her happiness at having escaped from
her life in London seemed to have evaporated,
leaving her feeling as flat as a half-opened can of
Coca-Cola. She was not really concentrating as she
pulled in to park in front of the long, low building
of the hotel, and didn't notice the other car in front
of her until it was too late. It, too, had pulled in
to park, and she misjudged the distance between
them. It wasn't much of a bump, but two accidents
in one day! Hurriedly she reversed, then finished
parking. Feeling extremely guilty, she got out to
face the other driver.

'Oh, no!' She looked up into the sardonic face
of the man who drove the Ferrari. Her heart began
to thump uncomfortably as he raised one eyebrow
at her discomfort.

'Trying to get your revenge?' he enquired lightly,
before moving forward to check if there was any
damage. She bit her lip in frustration. Of all the
cars and people in France, why did she have to hit
his?

'I'm terribly sorry,' she apologised lamely,
moving over to join him. 'Have I done any
damage?'

'None that I can see, we've both been luckier this time! Look, you just caught my rear bumper. What about your car?'

Still furious with herself, she turned to look, running her hand lightly over the bright blue paint. 'No, my car seems to be all right too...' Her voice sounded wobbly and unlike herself. 'I'm really terribly sorry, I didn't see you.'

'I expect you're tired. It's been a long day, hasn't it?' Surprised, she looked up into his face to see he was smiling at her, still with one eyebrow quizzically raised. 'Anyway, you've got nothing to be sorry about, no harm's been done.' He looked carefully at the Escort. 'I see you've had your light mended. No problems, I hope?'

'What? Oh, yes, thank you...' She put up one hand wearily to her head. 'By the way, I owe you some money, you gave me far too much. I tried to find you on the boat to return it, but no luck.' She had been fumbling in her bag as she spoke, and withdrew the remaining notes that he had given her that morning. 'You were too generous...' She held the money out to him, not too sure about the rather cynical smile that was on his face.

'That was for the trouble I caused you,' he said smoothly. 'You'd better keep it.' The shock was beginning to wear off, and Lucy felt more like herself as she raised her chin in unspoken challenge. She allowed an expression of surprise to cross her face.

'Keep it? Whatever for? I've had my car mended.'

Rather reluctantly he took the crumpled notes from her outstretched hand. 'I've got a better idea. Why don't you let me buy you dinner? That is . . .' his eyes assessed her carefully, 'if you aren't already meeting someone?'

Lucy wasn't sure she liked the expression on his face, and her doubt showed.

'This seems an appropriate way to make amends, doesn't it?' He looked down at the notes in his hand rather ruefully before raising his head to give her a charming smile. 'My name is JJ O'Donnell, by the way, and I can assure you I'm perfectly respectable, even house-trained.'

She heard the query in his voice, but shock at hearing his name had made her mouth drop open in surprise, and his eyes narrowed at her expression.

'I see you know of me, but why the expression of horror?' he asked lightly. She tried valiantly to pull herself together and ignore the jumbled thoughts careering around her mind.

'No horror,' she answered, equally lightly, 'just surprise, that's all. I heard your name mentioned for the first time today, something about developing land . . .' she waved her arms vaguely ' . . . so it is a bit disconcerting to meet you like this.' She was quick to notice that he didn't look as if he altogether believed her, but he seemed prepared to let it go.

'And you? What is your name?' She had a sudden conviction that it would be better if he didn't learn her real name.

'Lucy—er—Smith,' she replied, hoping he wouldn't notice how difficult she found it to lie.

'Well, Lucy—er—Smith, may I help you with your luggage?' She blushed scarlet under his cynical appraisal, knowing that he was perfectly aware her name was not Smith. She was made even more uncomfortable when he took her bags from the car and there were the initials L. P. on her cases, clearly compounding her folly.

He walked over with her to the *concierge*'s desk as she was frantically trying to think up some excuse to explain why Lucy Porter had suddenly become Lucy Smith. His smile was definitely unkind as he looked down into her face.

'I've already checked in, so I'll leave you now... Shall we meet in the bar, say, in an hour and a half? I'm sure you won't want to eat late this evening, as you're tired.'

She was torn between gratitude and shame, and tried to make amends. 'My name isn't really Smith...' she started to explain, but he held up a hand to stop her.

'Don't bother to explain! We are, after all, only ships that pass in the night, and Lucy is fine by me!' He gave her a languid salute. 'See you later.' And he walked away, leaving her speechless with embarrassment.

She was delighted to find, when shown her room, that she was to sleep in a four-poster bed. The printed cotton of the curtains, a fresh blue and white, matched the bed, and she guessed that the room had been only recently decorated. The whole effect was extremely pretty and simple, with co-ordinating paper on the walls and a matching blue carpet. The small adjoining bathroom had the same colour-scheme, and she lost no time in running herself a bath, using the complimentary bubble bath which came from an exclusive French perfume company.

As she lay back and relaxed, she decided that she would try to copy the decorating ideas for the bedroom at the farm, but not even her pleasure in the pretty room could keep her mind off JJ O'Donnell for long. She admitted to herself that he was definitely one of the most attractive men she had ever met, and she didn't blame Pascale one little bit for staying on so long in his employ... Pascale... She sat up suddenly and reached for the soap. If she wasn't behind Jean-Louis' ideas to de-velop the farms then she was a Dutchman, and that was why JJ was over here. She guessed that Jean-Louis had decided to take a week's holiday after checking with her family that she was on her way to Normandy, and if she knew anything about Pascale then she'd take a bet she wasn't far away either. She'd always had a healthy respect for the good things of life, and the money that was needed to buy them . . . Her hands stilled momentarily, and she dropped the soap in the water. Was Pascale trying to play for higher game? Jean-Louis' family were very comfortably off, but not quite in the class of JJ O'Donnell, if appearances were anything to go by.

She found the idea curiously unpleasant, and blamed it on her affection for Jean-Louis. All the same, it would be typical of the girl to try to keep two men in tow. If she couldn't quite manage to ensnare JJ himself then she'd try her hardest to benefit her fiancé from the deal. Lucy thought that subconsciously she had already recognised this fact, and that was why she hadn't wanted to give her real name, in case he already knew it and realised how important she was going to be to his future plans.

She got out of the bath filled with a new determination. There was no way she was going to allow Pascale to drive her away for a second time. Jean-Louis would get quite enough money from the sale of Grande Ferme as it stood, certainly enough for him to buy a house to start his married life, and there was absolutely no need for her to feel guilty. Pascale's greed was too well known to her for her to feel anything but pleasure in thwarting her plans. JJ O'Donnell didn't look like a man who would waste much time on forlorn hopes, and once he was made to realise that she had no intention of selling then he would give up and she would be left in peace. If she felt a small tug of disappointment that JJ would walk out of her life fast once he knew the truth, well, she hardly knew the man—they were, as he had said, just ships that passed in the night.

She walked into the bar later knowing that she was looking her best. Black silk jersey clung to every curve until the hips, where a short skirt of scarlet satin flared out, showing an almost indecent amount of leg. A chunky necklace in heavy silver hung round her neck, and matching long ear-rings swung from her ears. She knew every man's eye was on her as she tossed her long hair back over her shoulders and walked gracefully towards her date for the evening. He was sitting on one of the bar stools, and she slid on to one next to him, knowing that it would show off her legs. His eyes were amused and appreciative as he greeted her.

'Are you sure you're happy perched there? Wouldn't you like to move to a table?'

She shook her head. 'No, this is fine by me.' She smiled at the bartender who had moved in front of her.

'*Mademoiselle?*' he enquired.

'I'd love a kir royale, please...'

'Champagne and cassis?' JJ checked.

'Yes! My favourite drink, as long as I'm not paying for it.' She glanced at him under her lashes, but he still looked amused.

'I'll join you, although I usually prefer my champagne dry.'

She gave him a serious look. 'Of course, it would be wicked to spoil a really good vintage champagne...'

'I agree,' he answered gravely, 'but I hardly think they will use a really good champagne, unless I specially order a bottle, of course?' She knew he was laughing at her, but she just shrugged her shoulders and looked at him speculatively. 'Still, it might be fun to try it, all the same, don't you think?' Lucy couldn't help being a little shocked at such extravagance, but as she also still felt guilty about not giving him her real name she gave him a genuine smile.

'I wouldn't waste your money! I certainly couldn't drink more than one glass if we are to have wine with our dinner...'

'Another time, perhaps?' He gave her a glinting smile. 'Maybe if we ever have something to celebrate...'

She looked at him blankly as he gave the order for two kir royales to the barman in fluent French. She wasn't given long to speculate what on earth he had meant before he turned back to her.

'What are you doing in France? Having an early holiday?' He passed her a bowl of stuffed olives. She took one and tried to forget his previous remark.

'No, not really. My aunt died three weeks ago and left me a small farm on the coast. I'm planning to come and live here, I need a change from London.'

He looked at her with surprise. 'I wouldn't have thought a girl like you would be happy to live a rural existence!' he protested.

'Then you would be wrong!' she replied drily. 'You shouldn't judge by outward appearances, Mr O'Donnell!'

'JJ, please!' He smiled back.

'What do the initials stand for?' she asked curiously.

'Jonjo! A good Irish name!'

'You're Irish?'

'Not as far as I know, although my mother's mother was, which is why I was saddled with Jonjo! My father's family have been well established in London for at least three generations.'

'What are you doing over here? Business?' Lucy tried to pretend to be indifferent to his answer.

'Yes, I'm going to look at a property I arranged to buy earlier this year.' She was conscious all at once of an overwhelming feeling of relief. If he was already interested in land over here then he was hardly likely to want her little farm, and all her fears had been groundless. Relief made her smile widely at him.

'I love Normandy! We used to come every summer when I was younger. Of course, I've been told it's getting a bit spoiled now, too many holiday homes and hotels, but I still love it. I can't wait to get back . . .'

'Is that dig at me?'

She looked genuinely surprised at his question. 'Oh, no! Anyway, I don't know anything about your developments, except that you set up holiday complexes.'

He gave her a searching look, but as she frowned, puzzled by his manner, he smiled again. 'You'll have to come and see something I've done some time. We try to be sympathetic to our surroundings.' His blue eyes now held nothing but lazy amusement, and she wondered if she had imagined his earlier look.

'I'd like that. Don't forget I'm going to be based over here now.' She took a sip of her gently foaming drink.

'Whereabouts is your farm?' Although the question was asked idly, she couldn't help having the impression that her answer was important to him.

'It's a bit grand to call it a farm, it's more of a smallholding really, and south of Granville. Even if I told you the name of the village I shouldn't think you'd know it, it's too small!'

'Try me!' But before she could answer a waiter came up with two menus, and thankfully she allowed herself to be distracted. She was aware of his quick frown of irritation and was puzzled by it. Why should he want to know exactly where she was based? She was too experienced with men to put it down to an obvious wish to get to know her better. For all the charm and good manners, she was aware that he was deliberately keeping his distance. There was none of the warmth she had learned to expect from a man who was seriously attracted.

To change the subject, and to break the suddenly uncomfortable silence, she said, 'They say the food here is marvellous, and I have to admit I'm very hungry!'

'Good! Then I hope you'll enjoy your dinner. Tell me, what do you do in London? Model? I thought your face was familiar when I first saw you.'

'I write books for children. Oh, not grand ones, just little paperbacks which luckily have become quite popular, and that's why I'm able to live where I like.'

For the first time since they had met she knew that she had now really caught his interest.

'Really? How surprising, you don't look like a writer to me. You look far more like that American model who lives with Mick Jagger.' His eyes probed her figure teasingly. 'I should say that if you ever get tired of writing books, you could walk into a modelling career quite easily!'

Suddenly disappointed in him, she snapped back. 'Modelling is not an easy career! I did some before I was successful as a writer, and I can promise you that it is very hard work indeed!' He didn't appear to be too worried by her sudden spurt of temper, just gave her another enigmatic smile.

'So you couldn't be persuaded to take it up again?'

She shook her head vehemently. 'Anyway, I'm too old now...' He looked incredulous, and she laughed before continuing drily, 'You have to be a teenager now, and before you ask, I left my teens behind six long years ago!'

He raised his glass to her. 'Believe me, the years don't show!' The blue eyes looked warmer as he enquired, 'What name do you write under? Your own?'

'No, but if I told you I shouldn't think you'd know it. I do write for children, as I told you...'

'You might be surprised! I've got twin nephews aged four! They keep me pretty busy reading to them when I go and stay with my sister, and I do that fairly frequently; I love kids...' She got the feeling that he hadn't intended to tell her that last bit, because he looked a bit embarrassed. Liking him for it, she laughed.

'I love children too, although being an only child means I don't have any in the family. What sort of books do they like?'

'They have a pretty catholic taste, but I think their favourites are the *Tiger Tiger* series by Mary Bear. I certainly know at least one of those off by heart!'

'Do you find them amusing?' she asked curiously.

'Yes, I do! They aren't nauseatingly sentimental like some very young children's books, and I think they're fun. Luckily the boys agree with me.'

'I'm delighted to hear it!' she answered demurely. Once more she was conscious of having caught his full attention.

'Don't tell me you are Mary Bear?'

She laughed, rather self-consciously. 'Yes, I am.'

'Good heavens! I can't believe it! Do you do all the illustrations as well?'

'Yes...' She wriggled rather uncomfortably under his penetrating stare. 'The original Tiger was one of the cats at the farm I'm going to... So I suppose you could say that that's where the *Tiger Tiger* books started.'

'You have my sincere congratulations! When I tell the boys I've met you they'll be thrilled to bits!'

'I hardly think so!' she protested. 'They're too young!'

'Don't you believe it!' He stopped to study her carefully again, but this time she didn't find his scrutiny uncomfortable because of the genuine warmth behind his interest. 'I still find it hard to believe—I mean, you don't exactly look the part, do you?'

'What do you mean?' She found it a distinctly heady experience to be looked at by this man so warmly. He gave her a grin.

'Come on! You know exactly what I mean!'

She gave him an answering grin. 'I don't, not really! How do you think I should look, then?'

'Not a gorgeous, leggy blonde, that's for sure! How long have you been doing this?'

'Quite a long time. It was very hard to get started. Writing for children seemed to be an overcrowded part of the profession until I found someone who liked them. Lorissa, my agent, always believed in them, and she found a publisher willing to take the risk. We've done pretty well out of them so far.'

'In my opinion you deserve your success!' He raised his glass to toast her, the blue in his eyes appearing deeper under the intensity of his regard. 'So this is what you're going to do! Hide yourself away in France to continue writing?'

'Yes, that's my plan. London isn't right for me any more. I needed to get away, and what better place to come to than the one where it all started?'

'Won't you be lonely? Or do you intend to have lots of friends to stay?'

She shrugged her shoulders. 'I've never minded being alone. Perhaps it's because I'm an only child. I'm used to it, and in a funny kind of way I like it.'

'I suppose your looks make it difficult for people to take your work seriously,' he said musingly, as he rested his chin on his hand and looked at her. She was amazed that he should have seen so clearly what no one else seemed to understand. Because her little books were so deceptively simple, most of her friends looked on her work as no more than a beguiling hobby, not realising the amount of sheer hard concentration that went into them.

'You are the first person, apart from my agent, who has really understood that it's not easy to write for children! Most people think it must be dead easy.'

'I don't pretend to be an expert on writing books, but I do know that most things that appear easy on the surface are deceptive. I should think that applies to all creative fields.'

They had been so engrossed in their conversation that they had not bothered to study the menus given to them, but the gently hovering waiter in the background brought them both smartly back to the present.

'I'm afraid we're going to have to order now,' JJ told her regretfully. 'If we don't we'll lose our table, and this place really fills up in the evening.'

Lucy had little difficulty in choosing her meal. The speciality of the house was *'escalopes au naturel'* and she chose to follow it with venison and some of the wild mushrooms that are found so often on the menu in France.

'I see you're a girl who knows her own mind and her way round a menu!' JJ teased as she gave her order. 'In fact, you seem so sure that I'll join you!'

'Don't think you can fool me!' she grinned in return. 'You just happened to have chosen the same things!' She eyed him speculatively. 'You don't exactly look my idea of a stay-at-home type!'

'Judging by appearances, Lucy?' She laughed, but had the grace to look a little ashamed. 'Whatever I might have done when I was younger, believe me, there's nothing I prefer more than being alone in the evening. In my job I have to entertain a great deal, so I treasure my moments when I have to think of no one but myself!'

'I don't believe you! Why did you ask me to join you this evening if that's true?'

'Ah! But I never pass up the opportunity to get to know beautiful blondes!'

'Liar! You managed very successfully to resist my charms this morning aboard the ferry!'

'You can blame that on the fact that I'd had no sleep. I'd been driving through the night from the north of England to catch that damn boat!'

'You must be exhausted!'

'Not at all. I slept on the boat, then drove straight here so managed to sleep most of the afternoon as well. But, although you don't look tired——' here he raised one quizzical eyebrow '—I gather you haven't had a chance to rest, so I won't keep you up late tonight.'

Aware that she was suddenly feeling a bit breathless, she changed the subject. He was too attractive for her own good, this chance-met stranger. Now he had let down the barriers between them she found herself more and more under his spell. 'I'm so glad I didn't damage your Ferrari. I think they are the most beautiful cars in the world!' He looked rather amused at her words. 'Have you had it long?'

'This one, about a year. I do quite a mileage travelling around, so it's important for me to have a car I find comfortable and that has the acceleration.' He laughed softly at the expression of longing on her face. 'If you feel like that about them, why don't you buy one for yourself?'

'One day I will!' she promised him. 'But the books don't quite run to providing me with a Ferrari yet.'

'Have you ever driven one?' he enquired idly. She shook her head. 'You must try out mine, then...'

Her eyes lit up, then she sighed. 'If we ever meet again I'll hold you to that!'

'We'll meet again,' he answered carelessly, 'you can be sure of that...'

They were interrupted by the maître d'hôtel coming to lead them to their table, and as he started to talk of other things she wasn't given a chance to ask him why he was so certain. He was an entertaining companion, and the dinner was just as delicious as she had hoped. When she had stifled a yawn for the third time over her coffee she said, regretfully, 'I really am very tired, I'm afraid. If you will forgive me, I think I ought to go to bed.'

'I'll see you to your room.'

Lucy thought he had passed the waiter test with honours; the service had been superb all evening. He had only to turn his head and someone was at his side almost at once. She guessed he had arranged to have dinner put on his bill, and she hoped he had enjoyed it as much as she had. He's some man, she thought dreamily, as she watched him sign for their dinner. I hope he means what he said earlier about us meeting again ...

He looked up to catch her watching him, and his eyes crinkled into an amused smile. 'You look as if you're dead on your feet!'

'Thanks for nothing!' His words pulled her out of her daydreams. 'Well, perhaps thank you for dinner, it was great.'

'I'm glad you enjoyed it,' he answered smoothly, as they both walked out of the room together. She was amused to see how many women's eyes followed him as they left the dining-room, and she couldn't help feeling a little smug that he was with her. He took her key from her as they stood outside her room on the first floor.

'Goodnight, Mary Bear ...' His hands ran lightly over her arms. 'I rather like that name, it conjures up pleasant thoughts ...' His eyes looked intensely blue, and it seemed to her that his breathing had quickened. His eyes held hers, and one brow rose in query as he pulled her against his hard, lean body, and his mouth closed softly over hers in a light kiss. One hand traced the outline of her face gently before he pushed her away. 'You're rather a special lady, aren't you? Thank you for giving me the pleasure of your company this evening.' His mouth twisted into a smile as he fitted her key in the door. 'In you go, before I ask you to do something we may both regret!'

Half-mesmerised, she stepped into her room, the touch of his lips having completed the last disintegration of any barriers she had left after an evening spent in his company.

'Must you go?' she breathed.

A look of genuine amusement crinkled up the blue eyes. 'I think so, don't you? This isn't the time or the place.' He blew her a kiss. 'Until next time, Mary Bear...' Then he shut the door softly.

Left alone in her room, Lucy felt her cheeks fill with colour. Never before in her life had she invited any man to spend the night with her, and the first time she had, she had been rejected. Slowly she got ready for bed, torn between a desire to see him, and a wish never to set eyes on him again. She felt totally humiliated and wondered if he thought she said that to every chance-met stranger who bought her dinner. Slowly she moved over to the mirror and looked at her flushed cheeks and overbright eyes. Tonight she knew she looked as pretty as it was possible for her to be, and if that wasn't good enough for JJ O'Donnell then the sooner she put him out of her mind, the better it would be for her.

'It's no good chasing rainbows,' she told her reflection sadly, then got into bed and turned out the light.

CHAPTER THREE

LUCY was disappointed the next morning to find that the black Ferrari was no longer there. She took herself severely to task, reminding herself how busy she was going to be, but it was no good: most of her thoughts as she drove away were taken up with JJ O'Donnell and the disturbing way he affected her. In fact it wasn't until she had nearly arrived that she managed to relegate him to the back of her mind.

Cherrytree Farm had not changed as much as Jean-Louis had led her to expect. The high banks of the lane hid from view the sleek fat cows she knew would be grazing the rich pasture, but as she drove past Grande Ferme nearer to the coast the trees became sparser and smaller until she could see the grey-tiled roof of the little farmhouse ahead of her.

Marie's chickens were still running loose in the yard that surrounded the back of the house. She'd always found them more attractive than the English hens she had known because of their fluffy, feathered legs, almost as if they were wearing plus-fours. They scattered in front of her car as she drove in slowly over the rough cobbles of the yard until she switched off the engine, then they returned to their endless routine of scratching the dust for bits of corn. She sat quite still and just relaxed, memories from the past filling her mind.

There was a gentle wind blowing in from the large bay, and already she could just begin to taste salt on her lips. It was peaceful and totally familiar, and she knew she had made no mistake in returning. The housekeeper came out to greet her warmly, leading her in through the back door which she never remembered having seen closed, and into the kitchen.

Two enormous dried hams hung from the old beams with bunches of dried herbs and flowers, and on the walls were brightly polished copper pans. Her eyes moved round delightedly, noting little changes, but the heavy old dresser was still there, with its complement of blue and white china just as she remembered it, and lying in front of the stove was a large ginger cat.

'Tiger!' she exclaimed happily. 'You're still around, then; I was afraid you might have died...'

'Him!' old Marie sniffed. 'He's getting old now, so he prefers to lie there all day getting under my feet! The only things he chases now are the chickens when they come in!'

Lucy had bent down to stroke the ginger fur gently, and the cat responded by vigorously licking her hand in return, and she laughed with pleasure. 'You must be a very old gentleman now...'

Again Marie sniffed. 'Not so old, but, like all men, all he thinks of is his food and comfort!'

'Still, I can't tell you how lovely it is to find him here...' She sat back on her heels. 'Oh, Marie, I've missed it all so much, it's heaven to be back! Am I sleeping in my old room?'

'Certainly not! You will sleep in *madame*'s room, of course.'

Lucy's face clouded at the oblique mention of her aunt and Marie gave her a sharp look. 'There's nothing to fret about, child! She died very peacefully and alone, apart from me and the doctor, which was exactly what she wanted. You've no need to feel guilty, she didn't want any of you here for the end. She was never a person to make a fuss... Your luggage is in the car? I will carry it in for you.'

Realising that Marie had said all she was going to say on the subject, Lucy jumped up. 'You certainly won't do anything of the sort! I can manage quite well on my own...'

'Jean-Louis said he would be here to meet you,' Marie grumbled. 'But he is always late if there is work to be done!'

Lucy was too used to Marie's dislike of men to pay much heed to this comment, so she just laughed. 'Never mind, I'm happier managing on my own.'

'So I remember!' was the grim response. 'You always were too independent for your own good!'

'That's not fair!' Lucy laughed. 'Anyway, one thing is still the same, I'm a lousy cook!'

The old woman looked at her with a considering eye. 'That's because you have no one but yourself to cook for. Now, if you were married it would be a different story!'

Lucy grinned at her. 'I still haven't found anyone I like enough yet, and anyway I'm surprised at you! I never thought you would be encouraging me into marriage!'

'You are going to be fussy, just like *madame*! But you must not leave it as long as she did, you must have children of your own!'

Lucy was touched, and gave her a hug. 'Are you going to stay here with me, Marie, or retire? I know this is more your home than mine, and I want you to do whatever you want.'

'You are really going to stay here? I couldn't believe it when I got your letter... There is talk in the village about Jean-Louis selling everything up...'

Lucy sighed. 'Maybe he is, I don't know, but I want to stay here if I possibly can.'

'Then I will stay with you! Now, sit down and have some coffee, we can collect your luggage later. I have baked some biscuits for you; you need to eat, you are too thin!'

Lucy bowed before the determination and sat down meekly at the large, scrubbed kitchen table. She knew that she would be expected to give Marie all the news of her family, getting in return the local gossip. Anyway, the smell of the hot biscuits and coffee was more than she could resist.

Jean-Louis did not turn up, much to Marie's fury, and Lucy carried her own things up to her room. She wasted time gazing out of the window into the bay looking at the distant rock that was Mont St Michel. Idly she wondered what had delayed her stepcousin, but mostly her thoughts were caught up in the past until she was disturbed by Marie, who insisted on doing her unpacking.

Suddenly restless, she ran down the stairs and out into the small walled garden. Marie's news had upset her because it seemed as if Jean-Louis had made no particular secret about selling Grande Ferme for holiday development. According to the housekeeper the locals were divided about his plans—the younger ones thinking it a good idea, the older people more worried about the change it would bring to the area. The coast near them was filled with small, family hotels, very often with the same guests who came year after year. There were a number of new developments, mostly of holiday homes, but the particular area near her farm was still relatively unspoilt. Lucy knew it was probably selfish of her, but every hour she spent at Cherrytree Farm strengthened her resolve to stay and keep it all exactly as it was.

The sound of a car made her reluctantly make her way round to the back. She didn't feel particu-

larly like having a fight with her stepcousin at the
moment, but she knew she ought to make her own
resolve clear to him as soon as possible. She opened
the garden door that led on to the yard, then
stopped in astonishment. A black Ferrari was
parked there, and JJ was leaning casually against
it, looking around him with interest.

'What are you doing here?' she gasped. 'And
how did you find me so quickly?' He smiled slowly
and his eyes were very blue as they looked her up
and down. Nervously she smoothed her hair,
knowing that she hardly looked her best. She was
dressed in a simple pale blue T-shirt and a faded
denim skirt that was rather short, and she had not
bothered to make up her face except for the barest
minimum.

'A quick look at the register after I left you last
night made a few things clear to me!' She looked
at him with surprise and he gave her a sudden
frown. 'Come on, Lucy! You knew who I was when
I told you my name. Is that why you gave me that
long story last night about how precious this place
is to you?'

'No!' She was suddenly indignant. 'You lied to
me last night. You told me you had already bought
land in Normandy, so I thought you couldn't possibly be interested in my house!'

'Why were you afraid I might be?' he queried.

'Because my stepcousin mentioned your name to
me when we met unexpectedly in Rouen. He

seemed, well, upset, when he heard I wasn't interested in selling my little farm.'

'As well he might be!' JJ answered cynically. 'So this isn't a neat little plan of yours to try to get more money out of me?'

'How dare you?' Disappointment made her lose her temper; there was no warmth in his face as he looked at her this morning, just cynical dislike. Hurt pride made it necessary that she should make it clear to him that he meant no more to her than a stranger. 'Will you please leave?' she said coldly. 'I have no intention of ever selling this house, so you have no reason for staying. As far as I am concerned, any problems you have with Jean-Louis are nothing to do with me.'

'You're not going to get away with it that easily, my dear! I have invested a considerable amount of money already into this project and I have no intention of losing it!'

She raised her eyebrows slightly. 'More fool you! But I still don't see that your problems are any concern of mine!'

'Oh, don't you? What about that letter you wrote to me agreeing to the sale in principle once your aunt had died?'

She looked at him with astonishment. 'I have never written any letter to you! I didn't even know of your existence until yesterday!'

The sneer on his face as he looked back at her was strongly marked. 'Don't think you can get away with that! My lawyers looked into the matter carefully before I invested one penny!'

By this time Lucy was so cross that she threw all caution to the winds. 'Then they've made an expensive mistake, haven't they?' she retorted sarcastically. 'Let me repeat one thing to you! I have never,' she said slowly, 'ever written to you in my life! I don't like you, Mr O'Donnell, or your manners. Now get out before I call for help!' She turned on her heel to leave him, but she hadn't taken three steps before he caught her, spinning her round in his arms until she was facing him.

'You're not going to get away with this if I have to fight you in every court in France, Mary Bear! I don't like people who go back on their word, even if it's supposed to be a woman's prerogative to change her mind!' His eyes looked intensely blue as they held her furious grey ones, and she was outraged when an expression of amusement crossed his face. 'I'm going to win, so why don't you give in gracefully? We could have a lot of fun settling our differences, don't you think?'

His arrogant assumption that she would play along with his suggestion was more than she could bear. Quickly she flung up an arm and smacked him hard on the face. Furious once more, he let go of her in a hurry, one hand coming up to rub the patch of red that was already beginning to show on his cheek. 'That was a mistake,' he said quietly, 'that I think you'll regret.' He turned on his heel and left her, gunning the powerful car into life as he recklessly turned it before accelerating away to leave her once more alone.

Still furious, she stamped her foot hard on the cobbles. 'Arrogant, insufferable pig!' she stormed. 'How could I ever have thought I liked you?' Fuming, she turned back into the garden, still muttering to herself. It took her several minutes to bring her temper back under control as she walked unseeingly around the little garden. JJ's behaviour towards her so obsessed her thoughts that she was incapable of assimilating the one extraordinary fact that had emerged from their encounter until she had calmed down sufficiently to think rationally.

Who had written the letter to him purporting to be from her? It didn't take her long to come up with the answer, and she was no longer surprised that Jean-Louis had not come down to Cherrytree Farm to welcome her on her return. There could only be one person she knew who was capable of sinking to those depths to get her own way.

Pascale had never troubled to hide her contempt for Lucy ever since that last summer they had spent on the farm. To start with, the other girl had been furious at Jean-Louis' defection, and she had used every trick in the book to get his attention back to her. When she had succeeded, she then turned her attention to Lucy, quite unable to understand why she wasn't putting up more of a fight. She found it impossible to accept that Lucy wasn't very interested in Jean-Louis, and chose to believe that it was a sign of weakness. Lucy could have enlightened her, but did not to do so for Jean-Louis' sake. Whatever she thought of Pascale did not really matter as long as he loved her, and Lucy was convinced that he did and always would. The strain of trying to ignore Pascale's gibes, and also her step-cousin, without offending him, had made sure that she wouldn't willingly return while they still continued to use it as a holiday home. 'But this time, Pascale,' she told herself through gritted teeth, 'you'll find out just how wrong you were!'

It was well into the afternoon before Jean-Louis turned up, and one look at his face stopped Lucy from taking out her anger on him. He had come to find her upstairs in the room that Aunt Mary had used as a studio, and he looked totally shattered. She ran to take hold of his hands.

'What's happened, Jean-Louis? Has JJ O'Donnell decided not to go ahead with the deal?'

He shook his head in a dazed way. 'I'm so very sorry, Lucy, what a welcome you have had! If I had known or guessed . . .' He ran one hand distractedly through his dark hair. 'Pascale!' he said her name with loathing before continuing, 'I have broken off our engagement . . .'

Lucy's face softened immediately with distress. 'Oh, no! You shouldn't have done that!'

'But yes! Why should I marry a girl who is so greedy that she will even stoop to forgery?' He gave an angry sigh. 'It is partly my fault, I know. I should never have agreed to this long engagement between us, but I was still not quite sure that Pascale was ready to settle down, so it seemed better at the time...'

Lucy couldn't resist asking the next question. 'Is it because she is fond of JJ O'Donnell?'

He looked a little surprised at the anxiety on her face. 'JJ? I don't really know. Well, I suppose it might be... Does it really matter? She has behaved disgracefully, and I am ashamed.'

He moved over towards the window to look out towards the bay and the sand-dunes. 'I thought you really had agreed to sell, Lucy. That's why I was so surprised in Rouen when it seemed as if you had completely changed your mind. I called Pascale last night to warn her, and asked her to meet me at Grande Ferme... It has been a shock to discover the lengths she will go to just to get money...' He turned to face her. 'Even now she will not admit to doing anything wrong; she blames you for everything...'

'Does it matter very much to you if the sale does not go through?' she enquired.

He shrugged his shoulders. 'For me personally, no. It would have been nice, yes, to make so much money, but not important. We will get a good price for the farm when we sell it, even if it is not for development, although I understand that Mr O'Donnell has already got preliminary clearance to build on the land, so even if his deal does not go through there are bound to be others who will be interested.'

'What do you think will happen to Pascale when JJ O'Donnell finds out what she has done?'

Jean-Louis gave an eloquent shrug of his shoulders. 'Nothing very much. She took pains to point out to me that if I hadn't broken our engagement, then she was on the point of doing so...'

Lucy felt sick. It hurt to think JJ might have made love to Pascale's olive-skinned beauty, and Lucy dug her nails hard into the palms of her hands, trying to ignore the anguish she was feeling. She tried to convince herself that it was because she was so sorry for Jean-Louis, but a small voice inside her called her a liar, and she hurried into speech to ignore it.

'And you? Will you really be all right, Jean-Louis? It's been such a long time that the two of you have been together...'

Again he shrugged his shoulders. 'I think I have been very lucky. If we had got married two years ago as she wanted, then we would be in even more of a mess today.' He looked at Lucy's face carefully, then took her hand. 'But you are sweet to mind so much for me.' He gave the back of her hand a gentle kiss before continuing, 'Anyway, for the moment I feel as if I have had a lucky escape.' He smiled. 'At least it gives me a cast-iron excuse to stay down here with you for some weeks. Even

Papa agreed to that when he heard the story...'
His smile was now very warm and Lucy felt faintly
uneasy. She didn't want Jean-Louis rebounding off
Pascale into her arms, so her voice was matter-of-
fact as she answered.

'Well, that will be very nice, but don't forget I've
come here to get down to some serious work!' He
looked so dejected that she softened. 'But not all
the time...' He brightened immediately.

'There is a fantastic new restaurant that has just
been opened in Granville. The food is supposed to
be so good...' He kissed his fingers in an exag-
gerated gesture and she had to laugh at him.

'All right! But you'd better go and make your
peace with Marie, I think she had other plans for
me this evening!'

'No problem!' He smiled brilliantly at her,
showing impossibly white teeth. 'I will be back to
pick you up,' he consulted his watch, 'in exactly
two hours. Tonight we will forget everything except
what a great pleasure it is to see you again in France,
ma belle!'

Lucy was left alone with some very unpleasant
thoughts for company. Why had she minded so
much when Jean-Louis told her about Pascale and
her boss, JJ O'Donnell? He's a stranger, she told
herself, you don't know him at all. That instant
rapport you thought you had with him when he
found out you were Mary Bear was just wishful
thinking on your part. He might be the most at-

tractive man you have ever met, but looks are only skin-deep, as you've found out in the past, and you know you want more from a man... 'But there was more to it than that!' her heart cried out in protest. 'I know there was...' She bit her lip in sudden frustration, unwilling to believe that she could care so much on such a slender acquaintance.

Jean-Louis looked darkly elegant when he came to collect her, and he whistled in appreciation at her figure-hugging short dress. It was still cold in the evenings in spite of the hot sun during the day, and Lucy was wearing a dress made of soft wool, black, but covered with jazzy red spots. It was cleverly cut to flare from her hips, ending well short of her knees, and there was a short little jacket made of the same soft black wool, but without the spots, just with the edges of the jacket bound with red.

'Very chic, Lucy! Did you buy that in London or Paris?'

'In London!' His pretended disbelief made her laugh. 'We don't all have to shop in Paris any more to be smart!'

'So I see!' he laughed in return. 'But you are unusual for an English girl, Lucy; you dress more like a French one!'

'Chauvinist!'

'Not at all! I like any girl I take out to do me credit, and I appreciate it when they make an effort.' His eyes slid lower to encompass her legs and the low-heeled shoes she was wearing in deference to the fact that he was not much taller than her. 'I will be the envy of every man tonight!'

'I'll say this for you, Jean-Louis! You certainly know how to make a girl feel good.'

He kissed her hand. 'Plenty of practice!'

'I'm beginning to feel a bit sorry for Pascale, after all!'

'Don't be!' His voice was dry, and Lucy was ashamed of her sudden tactlessness.

They spent the drive to Granville catching up with all their family's news, but Lucy found it a strain not mentioning his ex-fiancée. They walked into the restaurant arm in arm, Lucy handing over her jacket before they were escorted to their table. She walked tall, with her usual lithe grace, knowing that Jean-Louis took pleasure from being seen with her blonde good looks, and enjoyed the attention she was getting from other men. She didn't always have to call such attention to herself when she walked into a room, but she knew that for all his charm Jean-Louis' ego had taken a bashing, and it made him feel better to be seen with so striking a girl.

She seated herself gracefully at the table, and as he joined her allowed her eyes to wander around the room. She stiffened with shock as she met the hot, blue stare of JJ O'Donnell, and sitting next to him, looking as if she could kill her, was Pascale.

Lucy tried to pull herself together as she turned her head to look at Jean-Louis. The sight of the two of them sitting together had upset her more than she would have believed possible.

'Don't look now, but sitting almost opposite us are your ex-fiancée and her boss!'

He surprised her by smiling warmly at her in reply, although his eyes looked furious. 'I know, I saw them when we came in. Try to ignore them, Lucy, and concentrate on me! Tonight you look so beautiful that I shall have no trouble in keeping all my attention on you...'

She smiled uncertainly in return, and although she tried her best to do as he said she was far too conscious of a burning blue gaze which she was convinced had hardly left her face since JJ had first seen her. There was really only one way out of the situation, and that was to flirt outrageously with her companion. Jean-Louis responded with such ardour that if she hadn't been already aware of his rage she might have wondered what she was letting herself in for.

The temptation to take a quick look became almost irresistible by the end of their meal, but it was something she was to regret. JJ caught her eye instantly, and she was horrified to see that he immediately got up from the table and began to make his way towards her. Immediately she started to talk in an animated way to Jean-Louis.

'Did I tell you that I stand to make a lot of money from a company who are negotiating to print some of the illustrations from my books on children's bedlinen and wallpapers?' Jean-Louis raised his eyebrows a bit at the breathless delivery, but he followed her lead with flattering attention.

'Clever girl, *ma belle*! I have to admit that I didn't realise quite how popular your little books had become...'

She tried to enjoy his admiring look, but all her senses were concentrated on JJ's silent approach to their table. She looked up coldly to meet his eyes as he stood in front of them.

'Pascale Rethel has just been confessing her sins to me. It seems I owe you an apology...'

Lucy interrupted him. 'Don't bother, Mr O'Donnell!' She stressed the formal words, her voice and face showing nothing but cold contempt; at least she hoped it was; it wouldn't do at all for him to guess the turmoil she felt at his nearness.

'Oh, but I insist! May we join you?' Without waiting for a reply he pulled out the two unused chairs opposite them. Pascale, who had followed him over, sat down gracefully, giving him a slanted smile of thanks as he joined her. 'Thanks to Pascale's over-devotion to my interests I find myself in a quandary...' The heavy-lidded blue eyes were fixed firmly on Lucy, ignoring the expression of frozen contempt on her face as she gazed back at the French girl. Jean-Louis appeared on the surface to be completely unconcerned, but Lucy knew that underneath he must be as disconcerted as she was by Pascale's daring to join them. He had stood up at their approach, but his expression then had surely made it clear that he, too, did not welcome them.

JJ took no notice of the frosty atmosphere, and spoke directly to Lucy.

'As I understand it, Pascale has acted very wrongly on my behalf, but in mitigation there was, as I'm sure you'll admit, good reason to think that both farms would be left to you jointly, and even when we discovered they were not, it still seemed likely that you would agree to sell. After all, it has been six years, has it not, since you were last here? I gather you didn't even come over when your aunt was so ill... I think Pascale can be forgiven for thinking that there was a strong possibility that you would be interested in my deal.'

'Maybe you have a point,' Lucy conceded coldly, 'but if that was the case, can you explain why she should have to forge my signature to a letter?'

Jean-Louis interrupted with a furious look at Pascale's strangely subdued face. 'I can answer that question with just two words! Greed and jealousy! She had the bright idea of concealing from Lucy just exactly how much you offered for her little farm! It was her plan to cheat her a little, because she didn't think it was right that Lucy should benefit equally with me! My God!' He gave an ugly laugh. 'You think she should be forgiven?' He saw Pascale's eyes begin to shine. 'It's too late for tears now!' he told her savagely. 'Save them for your new love!'

JJ gave him a startled look, and Lucy could have sworn that just for a moment he looked totally disconcerted. There was a nasty silence, broken only by Pascale's tears. Lucy stiffened with dislike as she saw JJ hand over his handkerchief to the girl sitting next to him, then he gently patted her on the shoulders. His eyes looked cold as he again studied Lucy.

'No one is denying that Pascale has done wrong, but...' here his eyes switched to Jean-Louis 'you mentioned jealousy... Don't you think that that is the real key to this sordid little drama? Pascale has told me that you two are childhood sweethearts and that once before Lucy tried to come between you... I think that is the real reason why she forged your name on that letter. She was afraid that it might happen again...' His eyes were now hard and cold as they raked Lucy's face. 'Judging from your behaviour this evening, I'd say her fears were justified...'

The shock of his words was so great that Lucy found herself incapable of answering. The injustice swirled crazily around her mind as she tried to come to terms with the fact that once more Pascale had managed to wriggle her way out of a nasty situation, leaving her looking as if she was in the wrong. JJ stood up and nodded to Jean-Louis. 'I'm sorry to have butted in like this, but it seemed important to try to get this mess cleared up. I stand to lose a

great deal of money if this deal falls through . . .'
His eyes, still hard and cold, shifted to Lucy's face.

This was all the spur she needed to pull herself
together. 'Then you'd better resign yourself to that
fact quickly, Mr O'Donnell!' she snapped. 'If you
think I'd sell my farm to you now, you must want
your head examined! I haven't the slightest interest
in anything you choose to develop. You're trying
to push me into feeling guilty so I'll go along with
your plans! Well, that little tactic isn't going to
work! I have done nothing wrong, and if you're so
besotted with your—er—assistant that you are prepared to go along with her criminal dishonesty, then
nothing would induce me to do a deal with you!'

If looks could kill, then Lucy would have been
dead, but as stormy grey eyes locked in combat with
the fierce blue ones in a battle of wills, Jean-Louis
broke the violent thread between them.

'Mr O'Donnell, you'd better come up to my
house tomorrow morning. There must be some way
out of this impasse . . . But I warn you now, I will
not tolerate any more bullying of my cousin over
this matter. She is well within her rights to refuse
your offer.'

JJ shrugged his shoulders in careless agreement.
'Very well, until tomorrow, then . . . Come on,
Pascale, it's time we went back to the hotel.' Lucy
was slightly mollified to notice that his concern for
the French girl seemed to have evaporated
somewhat as he left her to make her own way out

of the restaurant. After giving Lucy a look of pure spite, she turned melting brown eyes in Jean-Louis' direction, to be disconcerted again by his stony expression as he stared back at her. Again her eyes filled with tears as she got blindly to her feet and left the room.

'Forgive me,' Lucy said through gritted teeth, 'but your ex-fiancée is a bitch!'

Jean-Louis dropped his head in his hands. 'I know... I'll try to make everything right for you tomorrow with O'Donnell...'

'Him! I shouldn't bother. I couldn't care less what that man thinks about me!' She ignored the little voice inside her that denied her words. 'How he can be so stupid as to believe he has me beat? I thought he was supposed to be a clever businessman?'

Jean-Louis sighed. 'Surely you know by now that Pascale is adept at making men believe exactly what she wants them to?'

Lucy accepted the justice of this, but still had reservations. 'I suppose he is in love with her,' she said coldly.

'I don't think so, one would have had to be blind not to see that he has his eye on you!'

'Me?' she queried indignantly.

'Oh, yes! He couldn't take his eyes off you all evening... I have to admit I am intrigued... Have you ever met him before?'

She blushed slightly as she told him of their dinner last night and the way they had literally bumped into each other. 'He didn't know who I was then...'

Her cousin studied her face carefully. 'And you? You are interested in him, aren't you?'

Lucy exploded into words. 'No, I'm not! You must be crazy to think that! He's the rudest and most stupid man I've ever met in my life, and if he thinks he can intimidate me into making a sale of Cherrytree Farm then he's made a big mistake!'

'*Oh, la la!* Such heat, *ma belle*!' Lucy didn't like the slightly teasing look on his face as he watched her reactions, so she hurried to change the subject.

'I know I've already asked you this, but are you really sure you won't mind if the deal falls through?'

'I'm not sure if the deal will fall through if you'll be a little reasonable, Lucy...' He saw the mutinous look on her face, and put up a hand. 'No, listen for a moment, will you? If you sell your fields to me, then I think we can overcome the problem.'

'I don't want to have a large, flashy hotel built next to my house!' she spat back.

'Wait a moment, you little spitfire! This isn't my plan. O'Donnell will have to try to do a deal with old Plouhec!'

This time her mouth fell open with surprise. 'You've got to be joking! He'll never sell...'

'He might. Did Marie tell you that his wife died last year? He's getting on a bit now, and I don't think he can manage there much longer on his own. If he was offered enough money I think he'd agree. If you'll part with a couple of fields, and I can't think of any reason why you want to keep them, then O'Donnell can build his hotel on Plouhec's land, farther down the bay. You could make sure that there were no houses built near you that way. We'd make it part of the agreement. This way his holiday homes on Grande Ferme have access to the beach, and nobody really loses out.'

'Why does he have to come here and spoil our bit of coast?' Lucy grumbled. 'I don't want hordes of tourists around me!'

'Be reasonable, *chérie*! If you agree to this then he's got nothing to complain about.'

A sudden grin split Lucy's face. 'I'd like to be a fly on the wall when he tries to open negotiations with Monsieur Plouhec!'

Jean-Louis shrugged his shoulders. 'That's his problem! Although I agree it could be amusing... A battle of the giants, don't you think?'

Lucy was silent, thinking out the implications of her cousin's idea. It was true that she was really only interested in the house and orchard, and the loss of the two fields wouldn't normally have worried her at all. In fact the only thing that really went against the grain was having to sell to JJ O'Donnell. She rested her chin on her hands.

'If I agree in principle,' she said, 'I don't want JJ to know until after he has made his deal with

Monsieur Plouhec, if he ever does!' she added cynically. 'That old boy will make him pay through the nose for his miserable little farm...' A sudden thought struck her, and it lit her face with inner amusement, but she had no intention of confiding in Jean-Louis. 'Let's go home, shall we? It's been an exhausting day for me, and I want to get up early tomorrow morning,' she pleaded to her companion. Jean-Louis was frowning a little.

'In a minute, *chérie*... What devilment are you planning?' There was a suspicious look on his face.

Lucy cursed the fact that sometimes her face showed her feelings too clearly, and pretended surprise. Deliberately she didn't reply too quickly, then said, 'Oh, you mean when I was thinking of Monsieur Plouhec and his meeting with Mr O'Donnell? You have to admit that will be very funny...'

He didn't look totally convinced. 'You normally only look like that when you are planning mischief!'

'For heaven's sake, Jean-Louis! I'm not a child any more.' Her expression of boredom and the sudden little spurt of temper seemed to convince him as she stood up to leave their table. Lucy kept her relief to herself, pretending tiredness as an excuse to keep her distance until she was alone in her bedroom.

CHAPTER FOUR

LUCY slept surprisingly well, although when she had gone to bed she had been convinced that planning her revenge on JJ would keep her awake. She woke early and stretched luxuriously before having a shower and getting dressed. It promised to be another lovely day, although it was still a bit cold this early in the morning. She added a thick Guernsey sweater to her jeans and T-shirt before grabbing a quick breakfast, then set off for the beach to find Monsieur Plouhec. The tide was coming in fast, and she kicked off her canvas shoes to jump over the incoming ripples that were spreading quickly over the sand—she'd always enjoyed doing that as a child. The wind blowing from the sea soon tangled her hair, but that didn't bother her as she ran swiftly in and out of the waves until she was opposite Monsieur Plouhec's house.

The old man was sitting on the wooden balcony that ran the length of his small bungalow, and he greeted her with a grin that showed missing and blackened teeth. 'Mademoiselle Lucy! This is a pleasant surprise, I heard you were coming back... You will have a coffee with me?' She accepted with pleasure, and curbed her own impatience as she listened to all his news. She commiserated with him over the death of his wife, and enquired after his married daughter, Lisette.

'She is very well. I have two grandsons now as well as a granddaughter!' He shifted his eyes from her face. 'As a matter of fact, Lisette wants me to come and live with her...' Lucy said nothing, just held her breath and looked a query. 'You are going to make your home at La P'tite Ferme like Madame DuParc?' he asked.

'Yes, that's the plan, I was always very happy here...'

He gave her a sudden fierce look from under his heavy brows. 'I have heard that Gilbert's young nephew is selling up his farm for development?'

Lucy made her face look sad. 'Well, that rather depends; the deal was supposed to include my house, you know.'

He snorted in disgust. 'Development! All they do now is ruin the land! When I first came here you could count the farms on two hands on this little bit of coast, and now look at it!'

Lucy pretended surprise. 'But aren't you thinking of selling up and going? I thought the same man who is interested in Grande Ferme was going to build a large hotel right here!' She looked at his growing fury with pleasure. 'Have I made a mistake? I must say, I would much prefer to have you as a neighbour than a hotel!'

'I have sold nothing!' the old man growled. 'Mademoiselle Rethel came to see me earlier this year...' He spat graphically over the balcony, and Lucy remembered that he had never seemed to have much time for Pascale when they were children. 'I told her then that nobody's going to make me move before I am good and ready to go, and I'm happy to leave that in the hands of the lord!'

Lucy smiled. 'I'm awfully glad to hear it, I was afraid the Englishman might already have bought your land now he can't have mine!'

'He has been speaking of this?' he enquired.

'No, I don't think so, but I don't really know. I only arrived yesterday, but he's already tried to bully me to continue with the deal...' Monsieur Plouhec looked at her approvingly, and Lucy was satisfied with her strategy so far, as the old man rambled on about how everything used to look. She managed to place one or two more promising embers on the smouldering flames of his anger before leaving, well pleased with her success. Let JJ try offering to buy his farm now; he'd be sent off with a flea in his ear! She knew very well that Monsieur Plouhec had a bee in his bonnet about building houses on good farming land. He was an obstinate, stubborn old devil, and if she was any judge of his character then he'd refuse all offers for some time to come. Just for a moment she had a sudden qualm. Maybe he would be better off if he lived with his daughter? Then she put the idea out of her mind. The old man was surely able to make his own decisions, and she thought he looked remarkably well considering how old he must be.

She continued walking on down the beach until she came to one of her favourite places: a single pine, bent almost double, and precariously poised almost on top of the sand which sloped deeply away beneath it. She sat down and leant against the trunk, hugging her knees and looking out across the large bay to the coast of Brittany on the other side. JJ O'Donnell seemed to think he could intimidate her, and she almost wished Monsieur Plouhec would mention her name when he refused his offer. She'd like him to know that he had her to thank for not getting his own way.

'Good morning, Lucy! You choose very early hours for your morning calls, don't you?'

Startled, she stumbled to her feet. 'JJ!'

He gave her one of his half-smiles. 'What were you trying to do, make sure the old boy won't sell his land to me?'

She blushed a fiery red. 'And if I was, are you surprised? After your rudeness yesterday I'd do anything to make you give up this deal!' she answered passionately.

'I really get up your nose, don't I?' he answered. 'You should be old enough not to resent the truth when you hear it!'

'Oh!' Words failed her, and she turned away violently to leave.

'Not so fast, sweetheart!' His hand shot out and caught her by the wrist. 'We have to talk!'

'Let go of me!' she spat at him, and as he dropped her wrist she rubbed it as if somehow she could remove the feeling of his fingers on her skin.

'Is Jean-Louis DuParc the reason why you have chosen to come and live in Normandy?'

In her fury she forgot all caution. 'Hardly! I'd have chosen Paris if I'd had that in mind!' she snapped. 'Anyway, what business is it of yours?'

'I was thinking of Pascale Rethel!'

'Really?' she sneered. 'And you, of course, know her so well, don't you?'

He gave her a look of contempt. 'Not in the sense you mean! I'm merely concerned that her future happiness should not be spoilt!'

She folded her arms and studied him insolently, her eyes running over the good-looking face then down his tall, lithe body. He too was wearing jeans, beautifully cut, that moulded his figure, and a loose-weave blue cotton shirt that almost matched his eyes. A navy jersey, not unlike hers, was tied loosely around his neck. 'You look as if you should be modelling men's fashions,' she said sarcastically, 'and don't tell me some woman didn't buy that shirt for you because I wouldn't believe it! I can just hear her saying, "It matches your eyes, darling!"' A dull colour rose up under his skin and Lucy knew that for once she had totally disconcerted him. Intent on keeping the initiative, she continued scornfully, 'You really have a high opinion of yourself, don't you? "Always right" O'Donnell! You decided right from the moment of first meeting me that I was a bitch, and you were only too ready to believe whatever Pascale told you! I don't know what you've got against girls who look like me, and I don't particularly care, but this time you're wrong!'

'All right, then, prove it to me!'

It was Lucy's turn to be disconcerted. 'Prove it to you?' she queried.

'Yes! Send Jean-Louis back to Paris. I know you can do it!'

'Why on earth should I?' she countered. 'Anyway, he's not a child to be ordered around!'

'You told me you were here to work! Is that a lie like everything else?'

'I don't tell lies,' she retaliated hotly, 'unlike your assistant!' He raised his eyebrows.

'If you want me to believe you, why don't you do as I suggest?'

She took a deep breath and tried to control her rising fury. 'I wish you would get it into your head that I'm not interested in what you think about me! And as for Jean-Louis' breaking his engagement to Pascale, I think he's had a lucky break! She always was a poisonous, scheming little bitch, and she's made him very unhappy by going to work for you!'

'I agree that that was a mistake,' he concurred, 'so I persuaded her to resign last night! She's on her way back to Paris right now.'

'Trying to shut the stable door after the horse has bolted?' she enquired sarcastically. He gave her an impatient look.

'No! I'm just trying to make sure that she doesn't suffer for the rest of her life for this idiotic mess she's got herself into!'

'How noble of you! I suppose you are quite happy to see Jean-Louis sacrificed in this cause?'

'Grow up, Lucy! Surely you can see, whatever faults they may both have, they are right for each other?'

'Jean-Louis is far too nice to have to spend the rest of his life tied to Pascale!'

He gave an impatient sigh. 'Look, can't you see that he needs someone tough behind him? Or are you so besotted that you can't think straight?'

'Two days ago I have never heard of you! As you so rightly pointed out that evening in Caen, we were ships that passed in the night. I don't know what right you think you have to try and dictate my life to me! You're arrogant and bossy and a total stranger, and the sooner you get used to the fact that I've no intention of letting you play God in my life, the happier I will be!'

'We're not destined to remain strangers, as you know very well!' he said savagely, then pulled her into his arms. She strained every nerve in her body to resist his passionate assault as his mouth caught hers, but he was too strong for her. The feel of his body pressed against hers was electrifying. Terrified at the feelings he was evoking in her, she tried to pull away. He let her go with a suddenness that was almost shocking. His breathing was erratic and he looked shaken. She moved away, looking at him with wide, shocked eyes, and put up a hand to rub her mouth.

'Don't ever touch me again!' she said, in a trembling voice.

'I'm sorry, I didn't intend that to happen...' he muttered.

'Don't pretend you're sorry! Just leave me alone!' She almost screamed the words at him, then turned to run back along the beach as if she was being chased by all the devils in hell.

Arrogant bastard, she told herself, why did he have to be right? She knew, she had always known of the link that bound Jean-Louis and Pascale together, that was why she had never returned to the farm. But it wasn't her stepcousin's affairs that concentrated her mind. There was a bitter feeling of satisfaction that JJ was as aware of the attraction between them as she was. Hateful, bossy— why should she be so aware of him? She hardly knew the man, yet part of her had seemed to recognise him instantly. He must not be allowed to get the better of her, even if she had to violate her conviction that he was going to be of importance in her life.

Jean-Louis found her late that afternoon in the yard. She had been making pen and ink sketches of Marie's hens.

'But, Lucy, these are enchanting...' His hands moved expressively. 'They look so real, as if I could touch them.'

She was amused that he could not find words to express his enthusiasm properly. 'If you like the sketches that much, then take them.'

He looked at her incredulously. 'You do not want them?'

'No, I was just trying to get my eye in before getting down to some serious work.'

'But they must be mounted and framed!'

She raised her eyebrows in surprise. 'Come on! They're only sketches, nothing important...'

'They are so comic and amusing! You have a gift *chérie*, more than you give yourself credit for...'

'There's nothing "great" about my work, Jean-Louis. I'm lucky, that's all. Heavens, I know plenty of people who draw better than I do!'

He concentrated on her work carefully, turning over the sketches, studying her technique. 'You should not denigrate yourself so, but even if you are not a "great" artist in the accepted sense, there is an originality about your work...' He waved his arms, as if trying to find the right words. 'I have never considered hens before. To me they have always been rather stupid birds, a collection of feathers good for only two things: eggs, and, if they are properly cooked, a meal; but now it will never be the same again! You have given them character, made them live for me...'

She laughed, then looked at her work critically. 'I had no idea I was creating anything so earth-shaking!' she teased.

He put a careless arm about her shoulders. 'You have finished?'

She nodded.

'Then let us go and talk, I have a lot to tell you!'

Lucy felt herself tense, but there was nothing she could do to avoid listening to his plans. Her early meeting with JJ had shattered her so much that she had deliberately not allowed herself to dwell on it, taking refuge in the one thing that concentrated her mind, her drawing. Unconsciously she gave a big sigh.

'It's all going to work out, *ma belle*! You don't need to worry!' She knew that as far as she was concerned JJ spelt trouble, but as she couldn't exactly give him her reasons for thinking so she kept quiet as she led him into the conservatory that ran the length of the house.

She could see his excitement as he sat down with her at the old wrought-iron circular table.

'O'Donnell wants to continue with the deal!' Lucy looked into his sparkling eyes and knew she had been naïve to underestimate the power of money. 'Once we had worked out everything to our satisfaction we went on to meet old Plouhec, and he has agreed to sell his farm to O'Donnell as well!'

This news did make her mouth drop open in surprise and horror, but luckily Jean-Louis continued before she had a chance to put her foot in it. He gave a delighted laugh at her expression.

'You might well look amazed, but JJ handled the whole affair beautifully! To start with, the old boy was breathing fire about all developers, but JJ showed him the plans for Grande Ferme and that soon calmed him down. In fact he was quite interested, and in no time they were exchanging ideas. It was crazy seeing the two of them talking away as if they'd known each other all their lives. Anyway, once he realised that JJ had no intention of building some ghastly hotel over his house he became quite reasonable.'

'What is JJ thinking of putting there if it isn't a hotel?' she interrupted sharply.

'Of course there has to be a hotel, but it won't look as awful as we all thought.' He opened the briefcase he was carrying which she had noticed earlier. He spread out the large architects' drawings on the table in front of her. 'Look! This is what he has planned for Grande Ferme. Nothing is higher than a single storey, so it won't spoil the look of the countryside at all!'

Lucy thought that was going too far but, even biased as she was, she had to admit that it did look rather charming.

'He intends to do the same sort of thing on Plouhec's land, so although there will be one large, low building, it will be surrounded by these pretty little cottages and won't be the eyesore you feared!'

'I suppose it isn't too bad,' she admitted grudgingly, 'but I have to admit I'm amazed at Monsieur Plouhec's agreeing to sell.'

'He hasn't been very well, didn't Marie tell you?' She shook her head. 'He had a bad go of bronchitis this winter and he really ought not to live alone any more.'

'I thought he looked perfectly well this morning!' she snapped.

'Yes, he told us you had been to see him and were as worried as he was about O'Donnell's plans.' Lucy didn't want to meet Jean-Louis' eyes, unsure what the old man might have told them. She felt furious and chagrined that her plans for revenge had been so easily upset, but it seemed Monsieur Plouhec had not betrayed her, as Jean-Louis continued. 'I think he has realised for some time that it isn't going to be possible for him to stay there on his own. In a way he was rather grateful to JJ for forcing his hand.'

This made Lucy feel guilty, so she tried to change the subject. 'If he really has bought Monsieur

Plouhec's land then he needs my two fields, doesn't he?'

Jean-Louis' face took on a serious expression. 'He seemed concerned that there was a possibility that you would not sell because you don't like him?'

'He's quite right, I hate him!' Liking or disliking were not strong enough words to express her feelings.

'He told me you had a disagreement this morning?'

'Mr O'Donnell,' she spoke through clenched teeth, 'likes to try to play God! And if you'd heard all he said to me this morning then perhaps you wouldn't be singing his praises quite so loudly!'

Jean-Louis looked a bit worried. 'He did admit to me that he had behaved very badly as far as you were concerned...'

'I bet he didn't tell you just how badly!' she sneered. 'I suppose he's now worried I won't sell my land to him?'

'Lucy, this is going to be impossible if you intend to be difficult! After our conversation last night I felt reasonably secure in going ahead with the deal because I thought you had agreed to be sensible, but if you are going to allow your personal feelings to affect your decision, then I ought to let him know...'

Furious at what she saw as her cousin's pomposity, she finally lost her temper. 'You think he needs you to hold his hand?' she asked scornfully.

'Don't be such a fool, Jean-Louis; the man's a shark and well able to look after himself. How do you think he's become a success if he can't sort out his own problems? He can approach me himself, I don't need you to act as a go-between! Go back to Paris and leave me to handle this my own way!'

'Lucy!'

She ignored his shocked protest. 'Oh, go away and start to plan your wedding to Pascale! It's what you've always wanted, isn't it? If you chase after her now you'll probably be married in a couple of months; she won't be too difficult if you've clinched this deal with JJ!'

'But I thought you wanted me to stay here with you? Why do you want me to go?' He looked hurt, but Lucy hardened her heart.

'I've got too much work to do to concentrate on anyone at the moment! You know that's why I've come here, to get some peace and quiet! Anyway, hang around here after me and you'll find Pascale getting married to the first man who asks her!' He still managed to look miserable and she gave an impatient sigh. 'Look, I know you still love her, and always will! It isn't worth taking a chance now, is it? You know what she's like, she'll go and do something stupid to get your attention if you leave her alone too long!'

Jean-Louis suddenly collapsed. 'I'm really sorry, but of course you are right. I do love Pascale and always will, whatever happens...'

Lucy breathed a sigh of relief, then smiled at him warmly. 'You know, you'll probably both be very happy once you're married; you should never have agreed to such a long engagement.'

He looked at her shamefacedly. 'It's probably my fault she is so jealous of you... I have never let her forget how fond I used to be of you.'

'You are an idiot sometimes! I suppose I shall have to try and forgive her, then.'

'I wish you would, *ma belle*! It is only her fear of you that makes her behave so badly.' A sudden, teasing look changed his face. 'So, you are going to give O'Donnell a hard time, yes?'

Lucy's face closed up. 'It will be no more than he deserves if I do!'

Jean-Louis tried to look serious, but failed miserably to conceal his dancing amusement. 'I foresee an exciting summer ahead! Maybe it's a good idea that I have decided to go back to Paris—two's company but three's a crowd!' He blew her a kiss, ignoring the storm signals. 'I shall leave tonight, but I expect to be back soon with Pascale. There is a lot to do at the house, and we will have to decide what furniture to keep and what to sell!'

Lucy saw him out, then wandered off to be alone in the garden.

She had given Jean-Louis his marching orders, not because JJ had told her to, but because she knew it was the right thing to do. She'd always known that her stepcousin was under Pascale's thumb, and nothing had really changed as they had grown up. Deep inside her she recognised that the French girl probably cared for Jean-Louis as much as it was possible for her to love anyone, and that his breaking off their engagement was probably all she had needed to make her agree to be his wife very quickly.

There was no denying also that it made her heart beat faster to know that JJ would have to deal with her direct to get possession of her fields. The curve of the large bay meant that if he was to join his two properties he was totally in her hands, and the thought excited her. It was better that they should deal directly with each other. She didn't need Jean-Louis to shelter behind any more; she would face him herself, and whatever was between them would somehow resolve itself.

CHAPTER FIVE

LUCY expected to hear from JJ every day, but when a whole week had gone by with no news from him or Jean-Louis she began to feel disconcerted, then she got cross. That first day he had appeared to be in such a hurry to get everything sorted out that she couldn't understand his silence. She felt thoroughly unsettled, and wasn't able to work properly or concentrate on sorting out the house with Marie.

She tried to convince herself that it would be sensible to have nothing more to do with JJ, but the compulsion to see him again was too strong to be ignored. She found his face invading her dreams, however successful she was at banishing it from her waking thoughts. Her life at the farm had settled into a tranquil pattern, too calm for her turbulent thoughts. Suddenly impatient at the start of the new week with still no news, she decided to go into the nearest big town to have her hair trimmed.

It was exhilarating to be at the wheel of her beloved small car again, as the weather had settled into a pattern of warm, sunny days. Her bank account was looking surprisingly healthy, so she thought she might treat herself to some new clothes.

She had a successful day, and was just thinking of having an ice-cream and coffee in one of the bigger hotels when she caught sight of Pascale and JJ sitting together at a table set in a small café garden that gave on to the street. Almost without thinking, she hid herself from view behind a vegetable truck that allowed her to watch them without being seen. Pascale looked absurdly happy, and so did her companion. It was impossible to hear what they were saying, but it was obvious that the French girl was in tearing spirits. Lucy's heart sank down to her prettily sandalled feet as the pair got up and she saw Pascale throw her arms around JJ. She saw his tall, elegant figure bend over to return the exuberant kiss that was being offered and, shutting her eyes, she turned away, feeling sick.

Somehow she found her way back to her car, but all the fun had gone out of her day, and she hardly thought twice about the carrier bags full of pretty clothes which she tossed carelessly on to the back seat as she drove carefully home. How stupid she had been to allow him to manipulate her into sending Jean-Louis back to Paris! If Pascale was still staying in the area with him, then no doubt he wanted to make sure that there were no chance meetings between the two of them. Even so, her brow wrinkled as she thought it was strange that she had not heard directly from her stepcousin.

Later that evening, she went for a walk alone on the beach, trying to come to terms with the fact that what she suspected was indeed true. It wasn't pleasant to face up to, and as she walked, head bent, her footsteps aimless, she felt more lonely and unhappy than at any other time in her life. It was no longer surprising that she had not heard from JJ, it was quite obvious that he had other, more important matters on his mind. Negotiating to buy her two fields could wait, and she found herself feeling first bitter, then angry that she should have been treated so casually. She made a new resolve to make him regret that he had interfered in her life. She had been a fool, but it wasn't too late to make him pay for his mistake. There was Jean-Louis' unhappiness as well to take into account . . . She stopped and looked out to sea, but the beauty of the setting sun blurred in front of her eyes as they filled with tears.

Furious, she brushed them away, then turned for home, almost falling over a small dog that was sitting behind her. 'Hello! Who are you, and where do you come from?' She squatted on her heels to greet it more closely, then her eyes gradually narrowed in distress and anger. He was a small white mongrel with a black patch over one eye and a tail which she guessed in happier times would be curled tightly over his back like a teapot handle, but which at the moment was limp and bedraggled like the rest of him. He was terribly thin, but the thing that really got to her was the expression of beseeching entreaty in his eyes.

She looked up and down the beach, but there was no one else in sight. She could see from the tracks in the sand that the dog had followed her for some time. There was no collar and she stroked him gently with one hand. 'You poor little thing...' Gently she picked him up, holding him next to her chest, horrified at how little he seemed to weigh. 'You are coming home with me!'

She could tell that he was almost at the point of total exhaustion, but he gave one hand a tentative lick. 'It's all right,' she murmured, 'you'll be all right with me...' She walked back along the beach slowly, talking all the time. There was something very sweet and taking about his foxy little face, she thought, as he appeared to listen to every word although his body was racked with trembling.

Marie was horrified when she walked into the kitchen, and Tiger, once he had realised what it was she was carrying, gave a display of spitting wrath. Lucy ignored them both. 'Have you ever seen this little dog before?' she queried.

'Never! He is a stray, Mademoiselle Lucy, you can see from the look of him!'

'That's what I thought. If no one claims him I shall keep him!'

'Keep a miserable little scrap like that?' Marie sounded horrified.

'Why not? Is there any of that chicken left that we had for dinner?'

'You're going to give him my chicken?'

Lucy smiled slightly at the older woman's outrage. 'I must! Can't you see he's nearly starving? He must have a little chicken and milk, not too much to start with, we don't know when he last had a meal. Do help, Marie! I need a blanket...' She placed the dog down in front of the oven where he stood on trembling, shaking legs. 'He needs a bath, but not tonight. He can sleep with me...'

'You've got too soft a heart, like your aunt!' Marie grumbled, but she helped her to feed the dog, even adding a few drops of brandy to the milk and chicken. They washed the sand gently off his paws, and Lucy nearly cried when she saw they were cut and sore. 'God knows how far he's come,' she whispered. 'Have you ever seen anything so sad?' Marie grunted, but Lucy wasn't fooled, she knew she was upset as well.

She carried him up to her room wrapped in an old blanket asleep in her arms. He had wolfed the foot down greedily and looked for more, but Lucy had been too wise to give him any. 'Little and often! That's what is going to be best for you!' Twice more during the evening she had heated a little milk and he had drunk it greedily before falling asleep again.

He woke her up early in the morning asking to go out, and her last fear, that he might not be housetrained, was set at rest. She washed him in her bath, ignoring Marie's protests, and he became her constant companion, helping her to forget about JJ O'Donnell. She christened him Teapot because of his tail, and each day that went by he became more lively and happy. It was on the morning of the third day after she had found him that a letter came from JJ asking her to have dinner with him in two days' time.

Her immediate reaction was to refuse, then she thought better of it. She had to meet him some time, why not over dinner? She had every intention of being difficult, but there was no reason for her to make that clear straight away. Let him think that it was all going to be plain sailing to start with, then, when she refused his offer, the shock would be all the greater.

She noticed from the address that he appeared to have already moved into Grande Ferme, and she found her body gave an involuntary little shudder at the thought of having him living so near her. She gritted her teeth; she must not let him affect her so, and she allowed the image of him bending to kiss Pascale take possession of her mind. The fury this put her into made it difficult for her to work. In desperation she started to draw Teapot. She'd already noticed that now he was getting better there was a faintly nautical roll in the way he walked, and as she sketched him she allowed her fertile imagination to think about his wandering existence before he had met her.

In growing excitement she began to realise that she had the ideas for a whole new series of stories featuring Teapot and his adventures. JJ, the house, everything was forgotten as she began to work in earnest. Her new companion seemed to be perfectly happy to pose for her, he was still her devoted shadow, and luckily he was still too weak to need many walks. He was beginning to look far more as nature intended after a few days' food. Marie had wormed him and already he was putting on weight. His tail curled just as delightfully as Lucy had hoped when she first found him, and he was beginning to look like a well-loved pet instead of the miserable stray she had found. He had settled into a state of armed truce with Tiger, and if the hens that ran loose around the yard were going to be a different matter, then for the moment he was too unsure of his luck to push it in any way.

It was Marie who came up to the studio to remind her that if she was to be ready for JJ then it was time she stopped working and changed her clothes. More relaxed about her meeting with him than she would have believed possible a couple of days ago, she went to run her bath. Her long efforts at her easel and the writing of the first story in rough draft had left her feeling relaxed and happy. She had a strong feeling that it would be fun to show it to JJ to test his reaction, then she took herself to task for what she saw as her disloyalty. She owed him nothing, and it was better to keep it this way.

She tried, though, to take special care with her appearance, as she went through the ritual of dressing. She began slowly to come back to reality, and that was that there could be no future for her with JJ O'Donnell. Escaping as she had into a world of her own the last two days had been a poor preparation for what lay ahead of her this evening.

May had blossomed into a succession of beautiful warm days, and already the evenings were warmer. She chose a soft blue dress, demure, with a high neck that showed off her blonde colouring. It had a wide belt and a full skirt that flared softly as she moved. Already her skin had begun to tan, and she was the colour of pale honey where the wind and sun had caught her body. Teapot lay on the floor of her bedroom, watching her with interest. Already she had decided to take him with her this evening for moral support. She had taken time off her work to buy him a new collar and lead in bright green leather, and she had had his new name and address engraved on a tag, hoping he could never get lost again. He had turned out to be such a charming companion that she could not understand how anyone could have been cruel enough to abandon him in the first place.

She had asked Marie to show JJ into the conservatory when he arrived, and she was watering the plants when the old woman brought him to her. He looked suave and elegant in a dark suit, and when he smiled at her she had the ridiculous urge to forget everything except the power of his attraction for her. But there was a watchful look in his eyes, as if he wasn't too sure of his welcome.

She greeted him coolly, offering him a glass of wine, the expression in his eyes reminding her that he was not to be trusted. He accepted gracefully, sitting down at the table, waiting for her to pour him the drink. She was aware of his eyes probing the contours of her body beneath her thin dress and she was quite pleased when Teapot distracted his attention.

'Who's this?' The little dog was sniffing, half afraid, at his feet as he put down a hand.

'He followed me on the beach one evening; I think he's a stray.' She nearly poured the wine all over the table as she saw the way Teapot responded to his overtures. The tightly curled tail was wagging furiously and his whole body seemed to wriggle with delight as he placed his paws against JJ's legs.

'Well, well, you're a very friendly little person, aren't you?' Teapot rolled over on to his back and invited him to tickle his tummy.

'Teapot!' She spoke his name sharply, not at all sure that she liked this instant fraternisation with the enemy. JJ straightened and gave her a sudden amused look before accepting the glass she held out to him. He lifted it and toasted her silently with his eyes as she sat down at the table and poured herself a drink. The dog came to sit at her feet, pressing his body close to her as if her sharp calling of his name had upset him. She bent down to stroke him gently, trying to give reassurance.

'He seems an exceptionally friendly dog to be a stray,' he remarked. 'Have you reported him missing?'

Lucy stiffened with resentment. 'Marie has enquired locally, but if you'd seen him when I first found him you'd be in no doubt that he'd been abandoned!'

'How can you know for sure? He might just have got lost, and someone is desperately trying to get him back...'

Two hectic spots of colour stained her cheeks. She didn't know if he was serious or just teasing her, but either way she found his comments hurtful.

'Perhaps you'd like to report him on our way out this evening?'

'That's not a bad idea...' He had been watching the dog rather than her, and his eyes narrowed as he took in her expression.

In fact Lucy had been feeling guilty that she had kept the little dog for so long without trying to make any real attempt to find out whether he had been reported lost, but it didn't help her temper to have it pointed out to her by the arrogant man sitting opposite her. As usual he was blunt and to the point.

'I seem to have upset you?' he queried.

'Don't worry, Mr O'Donnell, I'm getting quite used to you telling me what to do!'

'Why the formality?' He smiled at her as if trying to break the awkward moment between them. 'You called me JJ quite happily in Caen.'

'Circumstances have changed since then. Anyway, as this is a business meeting it is better to be formal, don't you think?'

'Business meeting? What are you talking about?' He looked disconcerted.

'I thought this meeting was to discuss the sale of my two fields?' she answered sweetly.

He flushed. 'I had no intention of talking business tonight!'

She raised one eyebrow provocatively. 'No?' she queried.

'I invited you out because I want to get to know you better. You must have known that!'

'Why should I? I thought I made it clear to you that I'm not interested in getting to know you better!'

'Lucy!' He gave her one of his rare, heart-warming smiles. 'Look, we've both got off on the wrong foot with each other. I want to forget all that and start again! When I heard that Jean-Louis had gone back to Paris, I knew I had been wrong about you before!'

Furious, she got to her feet. 'How dare you patronise me? You might like to think that you're God's gift to women, but you leave me cold! I agreed to have dinner with you tonight solely to discuss business! And if I did encourage my stepcousin to return to Paris it certainly was not because you had told me to do so! I am perfectly capable of making my own judgements in life and I do not need you standing at my elbow telling me what to do all the time.' She gave him a smouldering look. 'I think you'd better leave, I've got nothing further to say to you!'

He looked white with rage as he too stood up to face her. 'You're behaving like a spoilt child! You don't like to admit that you are wrong, do you? You've got so used to men treating you as if you're perfect that you've come to believe it, and you resent my criticism which implies otherwise! I'm not an impressionable youth to be knocked sideways by your beauty and talent, and I've never yet let any woman trample over me as you seem to think you have the right to do. You're human like the rest of us, Lucy Porter, with all the faults that go with it. You're so used to men falling at your feet that you seem to take their total capitulation to your whims as a divine right!

'You're a beautiful girl, and if you ever learn that sometimes you make mistakes then you could be a lovable one! Don't worry about seeing me again, at this moment that's the last thing on my mind, so you can keep that fragile little ego of yours intact!' He whirled on his heel and walked out, slamming the door behind him as the crash of the wineglass she had thrown splintered against the wooden panels.

'You bastard!' she screamed after him as she was left alone with tears of rage pouring down her face. When Marie came to see what the trouble was, she turned on her. 'Don't you ever let that man into this house again!' she yelled.

'But—but why, Mademoiselle Lucy? He is so good-looking and charming...'

Lucy made a noise deep in her throat that stopped her in her tracks.

'He's a poisonous snake,' she hissed, 'an arrogant pig, rude, overbearing, pompous and a cheat!' She ran out of the room, leaving the bewildered Marie with Teapot.

'*Oh, la la!* What a temper, *petite*!' She picked the little dog up and carried him into the kitchen with her. 'But all the same, he is some man, that...'

Lucy didn't often lose her temper, but when she did she knew that the best therapy was violent physical exercise. She took off her dress and put on her old jeans and a shirt, then ran down to the beach. After running a mile at a good fast jog she felt calm enough to try to think rationally about JJ's accusations. The fact that he dared attack her after his own behaviour with Pascale she found quite mind-blowing. Well, she'd always heard that successful businessmen often lacked morals, and it seemed as if he was a case in point. Although why he should want to have an affair with her if he already had a relationship with the French girl was the most surprising thing. He hadn't exactly looked bored with her when she'd seen them together just a few days ago, and it was a lucky thing she had seen them. She felt herself shiver at the thought that she might so easily have fallen into his trap; he was hard to resist when he looked at her so warmly.

She supposed there was an element of truth in some of the words he had said, but it was twisted out of all recognition. Surely she wasn't as spoilt and uncaring as he made out? It wasn't her fault that so many men had made fools of themselves over her, was it? She'd always tried not to raise hopes when she knew that there was no possibility of her falling in with their demands. She realised that the frustration she was feeling wasn't going to get any better by just churning over his words in her mind, so she began to make her way home and prayed that she would again get so involved with her work that she would be able to forget him for hours at a time.

She was still working in her studio when she heard the telephone. Slightly dubious that it might be JJ, she picked it up and answered with a curt, 'Yes?'

'Lucy? It's Jean-Louis! I'm sorry to call so late, but I have great news for you!'

Her heart sank. 'News?'

'Yes. Look, I haven't got time to tell you now, I'm on my way down to Grande Ferme. Can you meet me there tomorrow evening?'

'No!' The negative came out strongly before she even had time to think out the implications behind it. He laughed.

'All right, *ma belle*, I'll have one last assignation with you at your favourite spot along the beach! The twisted pine at ten-thirty, all right?'

'But why, Jean-Louis?'

'Wait till tomorrow night! Look, I have to go...' The telephone went dead under her hand, and with a heavy heart she replaced it. He'd sounded almost happy, as if a great weight had been taken off him, and she guessed that Pascale had at last told him the truth about herself and JJ O'Donnell. She would never have expected him to sound so joyful, but maybe she had been wrong all these years to think that only Pascale had the power to make him happy.

Why he should want to meet her at their old trysting place had her a little worried, but then she shrugged her shoulders. If he needed consoling then she would be happy to help him up to a point, but he would have to learn that there could be no future for the two of them together, whatever he might think to the contrary.

Lucy and Teapot set out after dinner to keep their mysterious assignation with Jean-Louis. The early heatwave they were having had made it necessary for her only to add a light cashmere cardigan to the sundress she had been wearing all day.

The moon was only half full, yet there was enough silvery light reflected off the sea to enable her to see her way clearly. She had been tempted to call the meeting off, and only the thought that she might get JJ on the telephone had stopped her from calling Grande Ferme. She wondered how Jean-Louis could bear to stay there knowing that everything was at an end between him and Pascale, and guessed that he didn't want to jeopardise the deal that was to make him so much money.

The little dog skipped lightly at her heels, his pads better now that Marie had treated them with some old recipe of her own. A soft breeze came from the bay, and some massive banks of gorse behind her sent an elusive perfume into the night air mixed with the smell of the sea. The old tree showed up starkly ahead of her as she made her way to stand beneath it.

A soft whistle had her smiling gently; somehow she hadn't associated her stepcousin with such schoolboy behaviour. Teapot plunged ahead of her down the sand-dune towards the patch of deep shade beneath them. She followed more slowly, her feet sinking into the powdery, dry sand which filled her sandals then fell out in soft streams. As the velvety darkness enclosed her, strong arms caught and pulled her down on to the still-warm sand.

'Jean-Louis, you fool!' Amusement sounded in her voice, but she wasn't given a chance to say any more as his mouth closed possessively over hers.

Realisation came quickly that she had been tricked; this wasn't her stepcousin, it was JJ. Part of her was shocked at her body's response, but she seemed curiously powerless to prevent her lips opening under his. Immediately the kiss gentled and deepened, drawing her into a spiralling crescendo of sudden urgent pleasure. Her last rational thought was that never before had anyone else been able to give her such feelings of delight. She twisted her long, sun-browned legs around his, the thin cotton of their clothes unable to disguise from each other the burning heat of their bodies. His hands found the buttons that did up her sundress, and, unprotesting, she allowed him to slip it off so she was naked apart from her bikini briefs.

He spoke no words and neither did she as his mouth began to explore her breasts, his hands already cupping their perfect roundness. She murmured with pleasure as she lifted his shirt to explore the smoothly muscled back. Their bodies met and writhed on the dry sand beneath them, its soft slipperiness as it ran over her body adding further erotic sensations to the ones she was already feeling.

He smelt clean and fresh, and as she ran her tongue lightly over the slight roughness of his cheeks she could taste salt, as if he had been swimming in the sea and not showered afterwards. She felt his hands slip lower, so they cupped each round of her buttocks, and the sensual tension that gripped her had her lying expectantly beneath him, waiting for the burning touch of his sensitive fingers to explore further.

He rolled on top of her, letting the full weight of his lower body press her even deeper into the sand. She was acutely aware of his throbbing excitement as he placed one arm each side of her and raised his chest so he was poised above her, as if his eyes were now trying to pierce the dark to see her nearly naked body beneath him. Suddenly impatient, she reached up and tore his shirt apart to run her hands over the supple smoothness of his chest. He laughed softly, and her hands stopped their restless exploration. She had heard, behind the laugh, the satisfaction of someone who knows he has succeeded in attaining his goal. Memory took over from mindless pleasure, and her body stiffened in rejection.

CHAPTER SIX

LUCY tried to escape from the burning heat of the man's body above her.

'God! You're so beautiful...' The latent sexuality she heard made her renew her attempts to escape. 'Don't try to fight me, darling! You want this as much as I do...' The deep voice, now filled with overtones of amusement, made her draw in her breath with a hiss. The effect of his voice was electrifying and she started to panic. Her breathing had deteriorated into loud, gasping gulps of air, and she fought wildly for her freedom. Suddenly he let her go, and she rolled away to find her face being licked by an ecstatic dog. She groped wildly for her dress, and with fumbling fingers managed to get it on and buttoned up.

'Why the panic? I thought everything was going rather well...' There was still amusement in JJ's voice.

'Don't touch me!' Her own voice sounded unnaturally high.

'Hey! All right, I'm not going to touch you!' She heard the exasperated frustration in his voice. 'What's wrong, Lucy?'

Her whole body was trembling with emotion. 'You're a cheat! How you could...' Suddenly she felt tears pour down her face and she bent her head to give way to racking sobs. She felt a strong arm pull her to her feet.

'Come on, we can't talk in the dark...' He pulled her up out of the shadow into the light of the moon and sat her down against the tree that twisted above them. 'Now, tell me what all this is about!' He handed her a large handkerchief. 'Why am I a cheat?' He felt the shock of her surprise.

'You know very well...' She tried to control the sobs that were still shaking her body, then turned away from him to bury her face in Teapot's neck.

'No, I don't,' he answered quietly. 'Why don't you tell me?'

She tried to pull herself together, then blew her nose. JJ sat near her, but he didn't touch her or make any move to get closer. 'I saw you earlier this week with Pascale in Avranches!'

She saw the expression of surprise on his face.

'What's wrong with that?' It was her turn to look disconcerted, but she could see him watching her face in the dim light. 'She came down to tell me the news in person, that's all. She's getting married to Jean-Louis in six weeks' time and she's over the moon!'

'Getting married?'

'Yes, you idiot! What else did you think?'

'I—well, I...'

'You thought I was having an affair with her?' he finished drily.

'Yes! I couldn't believe...'

'Didn't Jean-Louis tell you anything when he rang last night?'

'Only that he had good news...' Her voice trailed away. He watched her as she seemed to wilt, all her proud strength melting away, leaving just a slender girl with a bowed neck and hair that seemed to take its colour from the light of the moon. Suddenly overcome by a moment of pure tenderness, he put an arm round her shoulders and tried to pull her close to him. 'Let me go!' she said tiredly. 'I'm sorry I misjudged you, but it doesn't really change anything, does it?'

He dropped his arm. 'What do you mean?'

She turned to meet his eyes, seeing a queer kind of hunger in them. 'I want to go home, I'm tired!'

His voice was gentle as he answered, 'I'll walk you both home, then...'

She shrugged her shoulders carelessly. 'You don't have to bother...'

She stood up and he came to stand next to her, putting his arm round her shoulders again. She tried to conceal the tremor that ran through her at his touch.

'I want to know what you mean!' he asked again.

She felt suddenly terribly tired, and, as it was easier to speak the truth, she told him. 'You want to go to bed with me.'

His arm tightened fractionally around her shoulders. 'And if I do, is that so wrong?'

'It is for me,' she replied. 'It's all any man seems to want from me.' He heard the bitterness in her voice. 'I can feel the wanting all the time; there's never time to make friends, to get to know one another, just this terrible pressure to submit...'

He drew in his breath harshly, but his voice was quiet, gentle almost, as he asked, 'And have you ever slept with anyone?'

'Oh, yes!' She spoke in almost a jeering way. 'Once, when I was much younger... I thought it would solve all our problems, but it didn't, it only made it worse...'

'Have you ever been in love?'

'I thought so once, but I found out I was wrong. He wasn't really interested in me. He just wanted his friends to know that he had been the first to "defrost me", as he put it...' she answered bitterly.

'Why did you ask me to stay with you that night in Caen?'

She sounded naïvely surprised as she answered, 'Do you know, I don't know? I've never done that before... Anyway, you turned me down!'

She heard the smile in his voice. 'Perhaps that's why you asked me...'

She hunched her shoulder disagreeably. 'That doesn't mean that I expect you to try and make up for lost time!'

'I know that now, Lucy...' He stopped suddenly.

She felt a sudden stir of curiosity and, because of what had already happened between them she felt no shyness in asking him, 'Don't you mind my turning you down?'

'No... Although I suppose it would have been better if you hadn't left it to the last minute! Anyway, why should I? I've never had to force any woman to give herself to me... She has a perfect right to change her mind at any time, as I have...'

Lucy was fascinated. 'And have you? I mean, have you ever changed your mind...'

'Oh, yes...' She heard a sudden bitterness. 'Men aren't really so very different from women, you know. I don't like being used any more than you do...' He squeezed her shoulder gently. 'I'd like us to try and be friends. Do you think you'll trust me enough after this to let it happen?'

She was intrigued, yet unsure of herself and him. 'Why?'

She thought he was smiling slightly as he answered, 'Because I was quite wrong about you, I had you written off as a tough little number on the make, but you're not, are you? You're independent and you want to make your own way in the world. You'd be the kind of girl a man could be proud of, an equal partner rather than a non-fare-paying passenger!' His voice sounded bitter, and again she was intrigued. She guessed that somewhere in his past there lay the answer to his involuntary distrust of her, and it wasn't too hard to guess that she had been blonde and not too dissimilar in looks.

They walked into the yard of the farm, and she was just going to ask him in when he stopped and tilted her chin so he could look into her face.

'Are you afraid of sex?' he asked abruptly. Suddenly shy, she tried to move away, but he stopped her. 'Is that the reason you've left London? Because you're fed up with being chased by predatory men with just one thing in mind?' She found the question uncomfortable, but tried to answer honestly.

'Partly, but not for the reason you think! I'm not against sex as such, but I've been very bored at being treated as a sex object, as if that's all I'm good for!'

He laughed softly at her answer. 'What a waste! So you've run away to take refuge in your childhood.'

Temper stiffened her, and she removed his hand from her chin. 'You have a genius for saying the wrong thing! Or is it deliberate?' she answered coldly.

'I speak the truth, but you don't like that, do you?'

'So you've told me before!'

He laughed again. 'Don't get mad at me, Lucy! I know I'm blunt, but I really didn't mean to offend you just now. You are running away, aren't you?'

'If you say so, "always right" O'Donnell!'

'I'm not blaming you! I've done some running in my life as well, but it isn't the answer. I wouldn't like you to make the same mistakes that I did!'

'What do you suggest I do, then?' she asked with deceptive sweetness. He wasn't fooled by her apparent docility.

'Well, you could help me this summer, if you've got the time. Now Pascale has left I could do with an assistant who knows the area. I am starting up a temporary office at the farm, so we could get to know each other, with no strings attached, and you could point out to me all the faults in my character, just to get your own back, of course!'

She had to smile, knowing that he was trying to defuse the situation between them.

'That won't be difficult! I'll give you some ideas right now! You're bossy, arrogant and too fond of getting your own way!'

'I could say the same about you!' he answered provocatively, and she gave an exasperated sigh.

'You are the most irritating man I've ever met! You seem to take pleasure in trying to cut me down to size, and if we're going to be together for any length of time we'll fight like cat and dog!'

'I don't think so, it takes two to quarrel! Anyway, I promise not to criticise you again. Shall we meet for lunch tomorrow?'

'That's going to be a promise you're going to find awfully hard to keep if past showing is anything to go by! And yes, you can come and have lunch here! There is something you can do for me in exchange, if I help you. I want to use you as a guinea pig for some new ideas I've had for my books!'

Once again he smiled at her. 'It will be a pleasure, Lucy!' He bent down to pat Teapot.

'And before you ask,' she told him, drily, 'I have reported him to the appropriate authorities. You will be pleased to hear that in their opinion he is a genuine stray!'

He grinned up at her. 'Yes, that was a bit below the belt! I'm sorry... If it's any comfort to you, you had your revenge! It's years since I lost my temper as badly as I did last night! That's why I was desperate enough to trick you into meeting me this evening. I knew after that fiasco you wouldn't willingly meet me again!' He gave her a rueful smile, then left her with a casual wave of his hand, saying, 'I'll see you tomorrow!' She didn't answer, just watched with mixed feelings as he walked lithely away from her.

She went back into the house, wondering just what exactly he intended by his offer of friendship, and why she had got into such a panic when she had discovered he could light such a fire in her body. He could be left in no doubt that together they were dynamite, so why had he decided to pull back so decisively? It would be wonderful to believe that he wished to build a more permanent relationship with her, but such a fantastic idea couldn't be true… She had learnt this evening that, in spite of all her convictions otherwise, he was a kind man who cared about others. She had only to think of Jean-Louis and Pascale to prove that. Not many successful businessmen would have forgiven Pascale for doing something so criminally stupid. He stood to lose a great deal of money if this deal went wrong. Just for a moment a suspicious part of her mind wondered if that was behind his wish to get to know her better, but she rejected the idea fiercely, unable to accept that that was all she meant to him.

Teapot ran up ahead of her towards the bedroom, and she comforted herself with the thought that, if the little dog liked him, then he couldn't be all bad. But, as was the way with all uncomfortable thoughts, it kept coming back to haunt her. He had never once mentioned his business to her after that first day, and in spite of herself she began to be intensely curious to find out why. He couldn't still think that she'd sell her house? No! He must know that she'd no intention of moving, but as she turned over to go to sleep she decided that the first thing she had to do tomorrow was to find out exactly how much of her land he wanted to buy. She had a good excuse. She needed his money to redecorate the house, she still had not forgotten how pretty her bedroom had been in the hotel in Caen.

The next morning she found herself too unsettled to work so she badgered Marie to give her a cooking lesson. The housekeeper wasn't too surprised to hear who was coming to lunch; in fact she seemed to approve of him, which immediately made Lucy suspicious.

'I thought you didn't like men!' she said to her.

Marie chuckled. 'Most of them I don't! Lazy, shiftless creatures, but there are the exceptions to prove the rule!' She gave Lucy a sly look. 'Anyway, here you are in my kitchen! You've never shown any interest in cooking the food before!'

Lucy decided to ignore this provocation as she wrestled with the chicken, which had to be cut into four pieces for the *Poulet à la Provençale* which she had decided with Marie's help would be within her limited capabilities. She'd already made the choux pastry for the cream puffs to follow, thinking that two courses were quite enough for lunch. Anyway, there was cheese if he should still be hungry, but she thought he looked far too active a man to be interested in long lunches.

Teapot of course was still convinced that anything she did in the kitchen was for his benefit. Although he was eating normally by now, he still seemed to be permanently hungry. Lucy realised that this was all part of the trauma he had suffered, but she knew that she now had to be firm with him, or he would turn into a thief, ready to grab whatever he could reach. They'd already caught him eating the hens' corn, and now he was better he was revealing his true colours as a born opportunist.

Luckily she thought he was too small to reach anything in the kitchen, and as long as they remembered to shut the larder door everything was all right, but she had underestimated his initiative.

Having finished cutting up the chicken, Lucy went out into the garden to collect some fresh herbs. She didn't notice that Teapot hadn't followed her until it was too late. On her return she caught him jumping down off the table with a piece of chicken in his mouth. 'Teapot! How could you?' He looked the picture of guilt, but his clever foxy little eyes were searching for a way of escape. Luckily she was standing in the doorway, so he was obliged to let go of the drumstick he had in his mouth. 'Don't you ever do that again!' She took it and washed it, putting it away in the fridge to cook for him later, sending him out to the yard in disgrace. He lay on the top step just outside the kitchen door, his eyes pleading for forgiveness, but Lucy was firm. She'd worked out that he had climbed on to the chair to get to the table and she knew Marie would never tolerate such behaviour. It was lucky she had just nipped upstairs and missed the sordid episode, otherwise Teapot would have found himself banned from the kitchen for ever.

In fact, trying to cook the lunch hadn't been a very good idea. She was still in the kitchen adding finishing touches, looking hot and bothered, when a casually dressed JJ wandered in.

'Good morning, Lucy! Something smells good...'

She turned to greet him, running her hand through her dishevelled hair. 'It had better be! I'm afraid cooking isn't my strong point. Marie has just been giving me a lesson.' She was wearing blue shorts, her long, brown legs bare, and a white shirt, rolled up at the sleeves, liberally splashed with tomato. He looked at Marie and raised an eyebrow in amusement as he greeted her, and she gave him a sly grin.

'I've been telling Mademoiselle Lucy that she'll never learn to cook until she finds a man!'

'Marie!' Lucy protested. Teapot, who had taken JJ's arrival to mean that he was once more allowed in, lifted his nose and sniffed delicately at the flavour of tomatoes and garlic. 'I thought we'd eat in the conservatory.' Lucy looked at JJ. 'You'll find a bottle of white wine in the fridge. Why don't you go through, and I'll join you there when I've tidied myself a bit?'

'Don't make yourself too tidy! I like the shorts...' He was eyeing her legs in a distinctly hungry way, and she frowned at him.

'I won't be long. Marie, you'll watch this for me, won't you? I must say I don't know how you manage to cook and stay so tidy!' she added with a smile.

'Practice!' Marie answered tartly. She opened the door to the fridge and took out the wine to hand to JJ. 'Now you both go and leave me in peace. I'll bring it out to you in about twenty minutes.'

'Bless you, you're an angel!' Lucy blew her a kiss and ran upstairs, followed by Teapot. She changed her shirt, and brushed, then plaited her long hair and put on a little make-up. She decided that it might be misconstrued if she sprayed herself with her favourite perfume, and following that line of thought immediately took off her shorts to slip into a thin cotton skirt with an elastic waist. She wasn't going to give him a chance to think that she was encouraging him in any way.

She ran downstairs to find him, but he had taken his glass of wine out into her small garden. She poured a glass for herself, then went to join him. He smiled at her, his eyes warm with interest.

'I'm afraid you've missed your stepcousin! He's had to get back to Paris with his loving fiancée!'

'Jean-Louis!' she gasped. 'I'd forgotten all about him!'

'He didn't seem to mind too much. He sends you his love and warns you that he expects you at the wedding!' He smiled at her again. 'We can go together if you'd like!' Her eyes had a slightly stormy look about them and there was a wry note in his voice as he answered her unasked question. 'I twisted his arm last night, you know! He didn't want to put you in such an awkward situation...'

She met his eyes defiantly. 'You're going to be a very uncomfortable companion if you can read my thoughts so easily!'

He shrugged lightly. 'It wasn't very difficult to guess what you were thinking, but the fault was mine, not his, so if you are planning retribution it had better fall on my head!'

Just for a second her mood swung in the balance, then she laughed. 'It'll probably be punishment enough to eat my cooking!'

'Nonsense! I have faith in my nose, and that told me it was going to be a delicious lunch. By the way, if you don't drink too much of that,' he gestured to the wineglass she was holding, 'I thought you might like to take my car out this afternoon!'

This time there was no doubting her enthusiasm. 'You really mean it? Am I insured?'

'You're twenty-five, aren't you?' he countered with a smile.

'Yes!'

'Well, that's OK, then.'

She smiled at him with pure happiness. 'You're very trusting!'

He raised his glass to her. 'I like to think I'm a good judge of character! You look too sensible to push it more than you're comfortable with.'

He seemed to enjoy his lunch, but she found she had lost her appetite, even though it tasted all right. He commented on how little she was eating. 'I think it's because I've been cooking it all morning!' she answered ruefully. 'Somehow you don't have quite the same enthusiasm after that.'

'I'll cook something for you one day! I'm supposed to be quite good...'

'Such modesty!' she mocked in reply.

'Well, all the greatest chefs are men, have you noticed?'

Stung, she replied, 'What about Elizabeth David and Constance Spry—not to mention Mrs Beeton?'

'For someone who supposedly isn't interested in cooking, you managed to reel those names off remarkably quickly!'

'That's because of my mother...'

'Tell me about your family. I know that you are an only child, but where do they live?'

He seemed to be genuinely interested in hearing about her background, and just for a moment she forgot her resolve to mention selling her fields to him. She waited until he had finished the pudding, refused any cheese and had relaxed over a cup of coffee before she brought the subject up.

'Why haven't you made an offer for my fields?' she asked.

He gave her a quick, calculating look before answering. 'I didn't think you would be exactly receptive to any offer I made you!'

She shrugged her shoulders. 'Ideally I would keep them just to protect the house, but Jean-Louis seemed to think that we could make a deal so there would be no building on them.'

He sat back in his chair and squinted up at the glass above him. 'When I first made an offer for this farm it was obviously with development in mind, but when you made it clear to me that that was not on, then obviously I had to think again,' he answered slowly.

'I understand that!' she interrupted. 'I'm not expecting you to make the same offer as you did before!'

He gave her an abstracted look. 'It isn't going to be easy if you refuse to have any buildings near you... I think the best thing I can do is show you the plans my architects have drawn up. You'll be able to appreciate my problems better when you've seen their drawings...' He stood up suddenly and stretched, giving her a warm, lazy smile. 'Anyway, I don't feel like talking business after that lunch! Let's go for our drive and leave it for another day!'

His refusal to discuss business with her left a little niggle of worry in her mind, but she was not proof against his lazy charm as he held out his car keys. She found driving his Ferrari an exhilarating and hair-raising business. Too firm a pressure on the accelerator pedal and the car leapt forward obediently, and it definitely got her adrenalin going with it. JJ appeared perfectly relaxed as he allowed her to find her way round what was one of the most powerful cars on the road today.

'Do you often let other people drive it?' she asked breathlessly after one fairly fast sprint.

'No. In fact you are the only person other than myself who has ever driven it!' She nearly came off the road with shock and pulled into the nearest lay-by.

'Had enough?' he grinned. 'You're a very good driver, Lucy...'

'You've just totally unnerved me!'

'Why? Because of what I've just told you?'

'Yes! I must say I was surprised at first, then I thought you must be used to the experience!'

He laughed. 'Do you want me to show you what it can really do?'

'Yes!' She opened the driver's door to change places with him and had no qualms about trusting herself to him. A friend of her father's who used to race cars just after the last war had once told her that if you allowed speed to excite you, then you allowed fear in, but JJ's controlled performance at the wheel allowed her to relax.

'Have you ever done any racing?' she asked.

'Yes, when I was much younger. Nothing really top flight, but I drove in the RAC cross-country rally a couple of times as second driver.' He gave a reminiscent smile. 'But I was never really good enough to take it seriously; anyway, I didn't have the money in those days.'

'Tough!' She grinned at him. 'But you must have been pretty good to enter.'

'It was a privately owned car, so don't think I drove for Ford or anything like that!'

She laughed. 'All the same, it must have been a thrilling experience.'

'Yes, it was. I was fairly crazy in those days, but you wouldn't catch me doing it again!'

'Why not? If you like driving that much I should have thought that it was the ultimate test, so why not go on?'

'Too much can go wrong. Anyway, my reactions are probably too slow. I've done it twice, that's enough!'

She breathed a sigh of envy. 'I'd love to do something like that! Oh, not the RAC rally, but something smaller.'

'Why not do it, then? Lots of women compete nowadays, and some of them are very good indeed.'

'I might one day, when I have the time and the money.'

He turned the powerful car down the lane that led to the farm. 'What about these new ideas of yours that you want me to see? I could look at your work, then we could go for a walk on the beach.'

'Haven't you got anything better to do?' she asked curiously.

'No, I've taken the rest of the day off. I've given myself a mini-holiday!'

Lucy watched his face a little anxiously as he looked at her drawings of Teapot and the text she had written beneath. It wasn't long before he started to smile. When he finished and looked back at her, she said, 'Well?'

She had perched herself on a high stool that she used when sitting at her easel, both hands clasping one knee. The warmth that softened his whole face as he looked at her gave her the answer, but she waited for his words, one eyebrow raised.

'I should say without a shadow of doubt that you are on to another winner!' His eyes lingered on her face as he handed the drawings back to her.

'What? No criticisms, no new ideas on how it might be improved?' She was so aware of him that she had rushed into speech, trying to break the spell that held her eyes locked with his.

He seemed to be aware of her nervousness, and his smile deepened, but still their eyes were locked. He took her face gently in his hands, and she felt herself go taut with excitement at his touch. Just before his mouth found hers, he whispered, 'You're a very clever and talented girl, and I wouldn't dream of asking you to change one hair on Teapot's head!'

His mouth closed gently over hers, but it wasn't a demanding kiss, and it was she who opened her mouth, as if asking for more. He pulled her into his arms, and she pressed herself close to him. The beating of his heart seemed to mingle with her own, as again she began to float away in mindless feelings of pleasure. His mouth left hers to seek the rapidly beating pulse in her neck, and one hand gently massaged the back of her neck, sending tremors of delight down her spine. His skin smelt clean and fresh, and her hands began to explore his soft, thick hair, as she too began to stroke the nape of his neck. She felt him tremble against her, and was aware of the heat of his arousal. His mouth sought hers again with a greater urgency, and she gave a little moan deep in her throat.

Instantly his hold on her slackened and he buried his face in the side of her neck. His voice sounded tortured and strained. 'I'm sorry, God, I'm sorry, angel... I never intended this to happen...' He tore himself away from her and moved over to the window to lean out and take great gasps of air. Slowly the world righted itself and she started to come back to earth. With trembling hands she bent to pick up her drawings which she had allowed to drop on the floor, quite uncaring, when he had kissed her.

She cleared her throat. 'I'm sorry, too,' she said, in a small voice. 'It isn't going to work, this trying to be just friends, is it?'

He beat one fist violently down on to the window-sill, then turned to face her. Distressed, she noticed that his face was white and strained and his mouth had thinned to a determined line.

'Yes, it will, because we both want it to, don't we?'

Her eyes fell beneath the hard glint in his, and she shrugged helplessly.

'I don't know, JJ, I don't know what I want!' She turned away helplessly, wondering why he wanted to deny what was between them. Never before in her life had any man been able remotely to make her feel as he did when she was in his arms. He had only to walk into a room and her pulse-rate rocketed. She was so intensely aware of him that it was going to be impossible for her to pretend much longer how she felt. She guessed that he wanted to give them both time before they plunged headlong over the abyss that their desire for each other had created, but it wasn't going to work, she knew it couldn't... There was only one way she could think of that would get them out of this impasse he had created for them.

She couldn't face him as she spoke, so she turned towards her easel, replacing the drawings on it, trying to think of the right words to tell him.

'Look, I think what's just happened has proved that we can't just be together and forget it! I know you are trying to do this for me...' her voice sounded unnaturally high and nervous, and she swallowed deeply before continuing, 'but it's an impossible situation, don't you see?' Her eyes filled with tears. 'I don't think I can stand it!'

He looked suddenly very tired. 'What do you want to do?' he asked.

She gestured to the drawings. 'I'll go to London to see my agent. I ought to, anyway, to discuss my change of plans with her...'

He gave a deep sigh. 'If that's what you want...' He started to move towards the door. 'I won't say goodbye...' She thought he looked defeated somehow; even the blue of his eyes seemed diminished as he gazed at her. 'But I'll try to arrange not to be here when you get back...' Then he was gone, running lightly down the stairs as if the devil himself was at his heels.

'No! You don't understand! I didn't mean...' But she was talking to herself, already she heard the roar of the engine as the big car was gunned into life and he drove away.

CHAPTER SEVEN

LUCY had a very successful session with her agent, who loved the new ideas. She also found that the wallpaper and bedlinen deal had gone through, so a hefty cheque had been deposited into her London bank account. Her agent also warned her that ITV were seriously interested in making a cartoon strip based on her stories.

A few short weeks ago she would have been over the moon, but now she found it an effort to show her pleasure. All she could think of was JJ, and the mess she had made of their last meeting. She had tried endlessly to rationalise her feelings; after all, he had only offered her friendship, even though she knew his body burned to possess hers. She had fallen head over heels in love with him, more deeply and painfully than she would have believed poss-ible. She had tried to contact him at Grande Ferme, only to be told that he had left and no one knew when he was returning. In desperation she had even rung his London office, leaving her name with his snooty-sounding secretary, who had refused point-blank to tell her where he was. Over a week had gone by since then, and if had ignored her messages then maybe he intended to write her out of his life as well.

She found she couldn't bear to discuss her feelings with her parents, and although she had told them all about the proposed new development plans she was careful only to talk about Teapot and Jean-Louis. Although she felt guilty about it, she was pleased her parents weren't going to be able to come to his wedding, even if it meant she would have to attend it by herself. She was fidgety and unsettled at her old home, impatient to get back to her new life at Cherrytree Farm and the possibility of meeting JJ again.

Certainly there was no word when she got back to the farm, only Teapot's ecstatic welcome to console her, and a letter from one of JJ's lawyers making her an absurdly generous offer for her land. Because she was feeling so guilty and miserable she agreed to everything that was asked of her. There was to be one building near her, a small café. She was a little upset, but realised that it was necessary to the whole design, so gave in. The only proviso she made was that it should be built as far away from her house as possible, and as this was immediately agreed upon, she signed all the papers and tried not to think about it too much.

Her next step on her return was to think seriously about decorating the house. If this was to be her home in the future then she wanted it to be as pretty as she could afford, and she was lucky enough to find a shop to help her in Avranches. They were enthusiastic about the commission, and once she had made the initial decisions she left it all in their capable hands. But she became increasingly restless. She made a good start on another of her small books, then decided to take a break. She rang Jean-Louis' parents and arranged to go and spend a long weekend in Paris with them. After her trip to London, Teapot had become more than ever her shadow, hardly letting her out of his sight, so there could be no question of leaving him behind this time. Paris looked beautiful. Although it was warm, the trees had not yet got their dusty summer look, and apart from the enormous numbers of tourists it was still the beautiful city she had always known.

She was surprised to learn that Jean-Louis and Pascale were to take her out to dinner on her first night, and wondered how the French girl would treat her. She needn't have worried. Pascale behaved throughout the entire evening as if nothing had happened between them, and everything was as it always had been. Mentally Lucy shrugged her shoulders, but for Jean-Louis' sake she played along with her.

It was Jean-Louis who wanted to know how she was getting on with JJ. 'He is crazy about you, that man, isn't he, Pascale?'

Lucy knew she would have liked to deny it, but even she admitted, 'He is intrigued...'

'Have you forgiven me for letting him take my place?' Jean-Louis asked mischievously. 'I didn't think you would mind too much, I could see how you felt about him!'

This was going too far for Lucy. She raised an eyebrow. 'As far as I know, JJ is very well, but I haven't seen him lately,' she answered coolly. The expression of dismay on her stepcousin's face was almost ludicrous, but it was Pascale of course who had the last word.

'He always has women chasing him,' she retorted, as if this was what Lucy had done, 'but he gets bored with them very quickly, as Lucy has found out!' She softened this remark with a sweet smile, but Lucy wasn't prepared to let it rest there.

'I suppose it is possible he might have got bored with me, but I didn't see why I should give him the chance!'

'Lucy! But why? I could have sworn...' Jean-Louis started to protest, but her wounds were still far too painful to be exposed to Pascale's malice.

'Maybe I decided I didn't want to be one more scalp to be added to his belt!' she interrupted tartly.

Pascale looked at her curiously. 'You know, I shall never understand you until the day I die!' she said dramatically.

Lucy laughed at her. 'Well, it doesn't matter very much, does it?'

She shrugged her shoulders. 'I suppose not, but still! To pass up such an opportunity! He is a very rich man, Lucy...'

'Ah, but I'm not looking for a rich man, Pascale! Just someone to love, who will love me in return.' Her face looked suddenly sad.

'I knew there had to be a man behind your reason for coming back to Normandy!' Jean-Louis said triumphantly. 'You fell in love, didn't you, Lucy? And it all went wrong...'

'Perhaps!' She smiled back. 'But enough about me, I want to hear about the wedding, and what you would both like for a present!' Pascale immediately became extremely animated, describing her clothes, their new apartment that they had bought, and how busy she was. It was left to Jean-Louis to answer the last part of her question.

'Pascale and I have decided that if you will do it, we would like to have two pictures, one of Grande Ferme, and one of your little house to remind us of all the good times we had there.'

Lucy smiled at them both. 'You're sure?' She was looking at Pascale as she spoke.

'But yes! If you could spare the time we would be very grateful, Lucy!' she replied sincerely.

Before going home, Lucy made only one expensive purchase in Paris. In the rue Saint-Honoré there was a very exclusive little shop that sold extremely expensive collars and leads and other paraphernalia for dogs. Of course it was mainly designed for the chic Parisian ladies and discerning tourists, but, for those in the know, those collars and leads were just as much a badge of success as scarves from Hermès or bags from Gucci. Lucy knew that her little mongrel was going to earn her a great deal of money one day, so she took great pleasure in walking him in and having him fitted with one of the smartest collars and leads she could find. She resisted the temptation to buy him his own four-poster bed, knowing that he would never use it, but as they walked out of the shop she told him, 'Now you can hold your head up high, Teapot! You are wearing what all the best-dressed dogs in Paris wear!' But her weekend in Paris had been a disappointment. She began to realise the truth behind JJ's words. There were certain things that one could not run away from.

She had been very touched by Jean-Louis' and Pascale's asking for her drawings as a wedding present, and as soon as she got home she started work. She chose to draw her house from the garden side, and hoped they would both approve. She completed it in a day, knowing that she wasn't going to have much time if they were to be framed and ready in time for the wedding.

The thought of going up to Grande Ferme without permission bothered her, but she'd heard from Marie that already the builders were there, so she hoped it wouldn't matter. For all her brave words to Jean-Louis and Pascale, she missed JJ with an aching heart that showed no sign of abating. If only he had not rushed off and left her that day so quickly, and if only she had not given him the impression that she preferred to take things slowly! Once she had thought that true, but the fire that he had lit in her had made a nonsense of that idea. For the first time in her life she knew what it meant to suffer from a physical craving that she had no means of assuaging.

She thought she had known that he was the only man for her from the first moment he had touched her in Caen, the night she had arrived. All her fighting with him had been based on fear that a stranger could have such an effect on her. It seemed to her that she had been waiting for him all her life, and that her body had recognised this simple fact straight away. She thought sadly how complicated she'd made her life by not following her instincts.

The next day, armed with all her equipment, and followed by Teapot, she walked over to Grande Ferme. She had chosen to start quite early in the day, and had had the forethought to protect herself with an old straw sunhat that had belonged to her aunt. Every week that had gone by, the weather had got warmer; although there had been a few spells of rain, nothing seemed to stop the inexorable rise of temperature.

Again she decided to draw the larger house from its garden side. She noticed that there were windows open and guessed that some of JJ's staff were using the house as a base while the construction work got started. She had seen no one on her walk over, so she settled herself near the shade of an enormous fig tree, but she could hear what sounded like bulldozers in the distance. It had been strange to walk over the DuParc land without finding any of the sleek, mottled cows that used to browse so contentedly on the lush grass.

She sharpened her pencils in preparation, looking round her contentedly. Aunt Mary's softening influence on the original rather rigid lines of the garden were obvious to her, and she gave a sigh, wondering what the late owners would think of this new change to what had been their home for so long. Apart from the distant noise it was remarkably still and peaceful; she could hear the noise of the bees as they attacked the low hedge of lavender that her aunt had planted at the edge of the terrace.

She made a start, her pencil moving with quick, sure lines, marking the outline of the building before her.

'Darling! Do come and see! There's someone sitting in the garden drawing the house!' The voice, high and rather fluting, carried clearly to Lucy's ears. Horrified, she looked up to see a vivacious-looking redhead hanging out of one of the bedroom windows. She was dressed in what was clearly a thin nightdress, and standing behind her was the shadowy figure of JJ.

Absolutely horrified, Lucy didn't know what to do. In her distress, she stood up to call to them.

'I'm terribly sorry for disturbing you . . . I didn't know you were here.' In a panic, she started to pack everything up, ready to escape from what was the most hurtful and embarrassing situation of her life.

'Lucy, wait!' JJ's sharp command stopped her as she looked up miserably again to the house. The redhead had disappeared, and there was no sign of JJ either.

He came running out on to the terrace in jeans, still pulling on the blue shirt which she had once teased him about. As he came near to her she felt her heart turn over with desire and love. He still hadn't shaved, but his virile, masculine body made all her senses leap into quickened life. She thought he looked rather white and strained, as if he had been overworking and not sleeping very well.

'I'm sorry about that,' he said breathlessly. He ran a hand over the roughness of his face. 'And for this! We didn't get here until very late last night. Viv will be down in a minute . . .'

'I'd better go,' she said stiffly, trying to ignore the ecstatic welcome JJ was getting from Teapot.

'Why?' he countered. 'She's been longing to meet you!' Lucy looked her amazement. 'She's my sister,' he told her drily, obviously aware of what she had been thinking. She blushed with embarrassment, and tried to explain what she was doing in his garden so early. If her heart had suddenly lightened from under a load that had seemed almost too great to be borne, she hoped it hadn't shown on her face.

'Pascale and Jean-Louis have asked me to draw both houses as a wedding present for them. I didn't realise you were here.'

'Don't worry, it doesn't matter... We saw them both last night in Paris. They gave us your news.' Just for a moment she could have sworn that he looked as if a memory had hurt him, but the impression quickly passed. 'I gather the new story has been accepted?'

'Yes!' She gave him a shy smile. 'Teapot's going to be famous!'

All the time they had been talking his eyes had been roving over her body with a queer hungry expression in them. She, too, had been unable to keep her eyes away from his smoothly muscled chest, remembering how it had felt under her exploring hands. She looked up to meet his eyes and was unable to look away. They were standing awkwardly in front of each other, saying nothing, when they were interrupted.

'I'm awfully sorry, my dear! I didn't mean to give you such a fright. I forget sometimes just how loud my voice is! It's all that shouting I have to do at the terrible twins!' She poked a finger at her brother. 'I see JJ has forgotten his manners! Can we tempt you to come in for some coffee? Or are you too busy to spare the time? I'm Vivvy Ames, by the way!' She held out a hand to Lucy. Her friendliness was so palpable that in spite of her shyness Lucy couldn't help responding. 'Why don't you go upstairs and make yourself respectable?' Vivvy looked critically at her brother. 'You're enough to put me off my breakfast.'

He flushed slightly under her teasing, but turned to Lucy before leaving. 'Don't run away, will you? I've got something I want to ask you.'

By now Lucy was quite incapable of voluntarily leaving his company, so she agreed to come into the big farm kitchen to join them both for a late breakfast. She learnt more about JJ's background in the short time he left them alone together than in all the time she had known him. Vivvy appeared to be a compulsive talker, and Lucy was grateful because it meant she didn't have to make much effort herself, just listen.

'I always like to come and visit JJ's new holiday sites if I possibly can,' she told Lucy chattily, 'but it isn't always easy to leave my poor long-suffering husband and the boys! But this time my mother has agreed to move in for a week. She loves to look after them, but spoils them terribly! I suppose it's because she's lonely after Daddy died... Anyway, it suits me! Anything for a break, they're quite exhausting!'

'How old are they?' Lucy asked shyly.

'Nearly five! And the day I can send them both to school all day is something I've been looking forward to for years! Oh, don't worry, I sound a bad mother, don't I? I don't really mean it, but they get into such trouble that it's amazing I don't have grey hairs already! Tom, my husband, you know, thinks I spoil them, so I have only myself to blame, but that's not entirely true! They have inherited too much of JJ's energy, and can hardly sit still for a moment, unless it's bedtime, and even then they have to have stories read to them!' She gave Lucy a sudden warm smile very reminiscent of her brother's.

'He's split on you, Lucy! I know you're Mary Bear!' The dancing light of amusement in her eyes was affectionate. 'I have every reason to be grateful to you, my dear! The boys love your little books, and so do I!'

Lucy shrugged her shoulders and smiled. 'I don't mind, why should I? It's nice to find satisfied customers. I hope they're going to like the new ones just as much! It's a bit of a gamble with children...'

All the time Vivvy Ames had been talking she had been organising the breakfast in the kitchen. The constant stream of words didn't seem to affect her efficient organisation, which was all the more remarkable considering the kitchen was totally strange to her. Lucy couldn't help wondering if she always talked this much, or whether it was a sign of nerves at meeting someone new. She also wondered just exactly what JJ had told his sister about her. At least she was being very friendly, so it couldn't have been anything too bad.

JJ joined them soon afterwards, having showered and shaved. Vivvy had been reheating the *pain au chocolat* in the oven, but on his appearance brought them out and placed them on the table.

'It's lucky your cousin decided to sell most of the furniture to us, we'd be sitting on the floor otherwise!' she told Lucy. 'JJ might not have worried about the lack of such amenities as tables and chairs, but I must say I was a bit worried at what I might find here, or what I might not, I should say!'

JJ smiled at his sister, but his expression was quizzical as he looked at Lucy. 'Has she drawn breath for a single minute since you've been together?' he queried.

'Beast!' answered his sister. 'It's a social gift being able to talk and make people feel at ease!'

'In your case it's more like a social disaster!' he riposted.

'All right, all right! I get the message, I shan't say another word.'

'That'll be a miracle if you mean it! How Tom stands it, I don't know.'

'He likes it.' Vivvy pouted at him. 'He gets worried if I don't talk!'

'I bet he does, he probably thinks you're ill!' he replied with brotherly candour, and Lucy laughed at them both.

'Are there only the two of you, or do you have any more brothers and sisters?' she asked.

'One sister is quite enough for me!' JJ answered.

'And one brother has been quite enough for me!' his sister retorted. 'He's bullied me terribly most of my life, and he still does, given half a chance.'

'If by "bully" you mean my stopping you doing crazy things, then you should be grateful to me,' he replied.

'Oh, I am, I am!' Her blue eyes, almost the same colour as her brother's, smiled mischievously back at him, before she turned to Lucy. 'He introduced me to my husband, so you see, I have to be grateful to him.'

Vivvy and her brother kept up a lively conversation with each other, so Lucy had little to do except smile when they became particularly ridiculous. She sipped her coffee and watched and listened to the two of them with envy. If only she had had a brother or a sister then maybe she would have been able to build up the same easy-going relationship. They were tidying up the kitchen when Vivvy turned to Lucy and asked, 'Do you like his shirt? I gave it to him for his birthday, and he's such a tactful brother that he's wearing it for my benefit today.'

Lucy had the grace to blush slightly under his sardonic look, as she told Vivvy that it was very nice and matched his eyes.

'That's exactly what I told him when I gave it to him, but I know he thinks it makes him look like a pretty boy!'

Lucy laughed, a little uncomfortably, not quite sure what to answer. 'Well, I've certainly seen him wear it before, so he must think it does something for his image.'

JJ wasn't going to allow her to get away with that. 'She told me I looked exactly like a male model,' he said smoothly to his sister, who giggled in reply. This time Lucy couldn't avoid the sudden rush of colour that stained her cheeks.

'That was only because you made me mad!' she retorted, her eyes kindling dangerously at the memory.

Vivvy gave her a mischievous look. 'That's a good sign.'

Bewildered, Lucy looked at her. 'What on earth do you mean?'

'That you get mad with my brother,' she replied. 'It's frightfully bad for his ego to have all these women falling at his feet! And most of them do, you know.'

'Enough! If you don't shut up I'll start to tell all the stories about your past . . .'

His sister made a face at him, but retaliated by saying, 'We've taken up enough of Lucy's time for today. I'm sure she wants to get on with her drawing, and you promised to drive me down to Mont St Michel once you've shown me the site.'

JJ asked Lucy if she would like to accompany them, but she refused, telling him that she and Teapot would be quite happy to be left in the garden if he didn't mind. Vivvy had run upstairs to get a jacket, leaving them alone. Together they walked back outside.

'Am I forgiven?' he asked with a faint smile as his eyes met hers.

'There is nothing to forgive,' she replied breathlessly, 'I'm just sorry that you misunderstood what I wanted to say...'

'I gathered that when I read your message last night.' He gave her a rueful look. 'I told you running away wasn't a good idea, didn't I?' She thought the conversation was beginning to get interesting, but, as she allowed her eyes to meet his, she was disconcerted to see that he appeared to have withdrawn from her slightly, and as Vivvy rejoined them there was no further chance for a private talk before they left.

Lucy was left with a great deal to think about as she started again to try to capture Grande Ferme on to paper. Vivvy appeared delightfully scatter-brained, but Lucy thought that underneath she was probably just as shrewd as her brother. She had realised that the other girl had been studying her carefully, for all her light-hearted chatter, so that meant JJ had told her—what? He had certainly moved with flattering speed this morning to make sure that she didn't leave in a hurry, but he had left her with conflicting messages. To start with, she had been sure that he was pleased to see her, but in front of his sister he seemed to withdraw, leaving her with the impression that somehow he was on his guard with her.

She sighed. Well, at least he didn't seem to be ready to leave again in a hurry, and Vivvy was to stay with him for a week. She thought it would be only common politeness if she asked them both for dinner one evening. Perhaps it would be wiser, too, to take care not to wear her heart on her sleeve. After all, JJ had never spoken one word of love to her... She bit her lip in vexation. All she had to base her hopes on was this tenuous feeling that they were communicating all too well at a lower, more primitive level.

CHAPTER EIGHT

ALTHOUGH Lucy saw JJ quite often the following week, he was never alone, always with his sister, and she had the clear impression that this was carefully planned by him. He was friendly, but all the time she was conscious that he watched her in a guarded way, as if he somehow didn't quite trust her. She found his withdrawal so hurtful that she, too, retreated into herself. Vivvy's lively chatter made it easy for her to hide her true feelings.

She learned a great deal more about his business life. She was already intrigued to find that it was quite usual for him to set up a temporary office near his latest development, although he was based in London. It was Vivvy who warned her that his secretary, Isobel Lamb, was on her way out to the farm, accompanied by some of his staff.

'She's a tough cookie! Guards JJ like a dragon, as well ... I don't like her much, I know she hopes to become Mrs O'Donnell one day!' She gave Lucy a laughing, sideways look. 'He's quite fond of her, though, because she's pretty good at her job and terribly efficient, but I don't think he realises how hard she's working to catch him! He takes her out quite a bit in London and we've all been quite worried that she might succeed one day...'

Lucy realised that Vivvy was giving her warning to expect trouble if she showed her face too much at the farm.

'This will be the first time that she has travelled abroad for JJ. I think originally he intended to use that French girl, Pascale, but of course she spoilt his plans by deciding to get married to your cousin! Anyway, no doubt Isobel is thrilled and will be making the most of her chances!'

Lucy answered with a slightly distracted smile— Vivvy's words gave her food for a great deal of thought—but she pulled herself together enough to enquire, 'When are you going home?'

'Tomorrow! JJ is driving me as soon as he has seen everyone settled here.'

After that Lucy didn't like to ask JJ if he still intended to take her to Jean-Louis' wedding. Grande Ferme had become busier and busier as workmen poured in, and she realised that he would have little time to spare for her. She said her goodbyes to Vivvy, then quietly took herself and Teapot away, determined to make her own plans.

She booked herself into a small hotel on the Left Bank for two nights. This time she knew she couldn't take the little dog with her, but Marie promised to look after him as she had before. The day before she was to leave, JJ called. As always the sound of his voice made her breathless, and her stomach tightened with longing.

'Lucy? I'm sorry to have left it until the last minute, but I hope you didn't think I had abandoned you? I've made arrangements for us both to stay at the Bristol. They can only let me have a suite, but you'll be quite safe!' Just for a moment his voice had sounded sarcastic. 'You can keep the communicating door locked!'

Hurt, she responded lightly, 'I'm quite sure I will, but you don't have to supply me with a room. I've already booked myself in somewhere else.'

'Then cancel it! There's no point in paying for an extra room you're not going to need.'

'All right.' She didn't argue, she'd heard the impatience in his voice. 'You will let me know how much I owe you?'

'No, I will not! You are to be my guest, so don't argue. Is it all right if I pick you up after lunch tomorrow, say around two-thirty?'

She agreed, and he rang off, as if he was in a hurry. Feeling happier, she couldn't help wondering whether he was planning to spend the evening before the wedding with her or had other arrangements, but, just in case he intended to take her out, she packed a pretty black silk dress that she hoped would be suitable, as well as her clothes for the wedding.

She had had her pictures framed and sent up to Paris, so had nothing to worry about except trying to organise herself instead of thinking of JJ all the time.

He arrived punctually the following day to find her waiting for him, but he was not alone. A cool blonde was sitting next to him in the front seat, looking very much at home with a shorthand notebook open on her lap. JJ got out of the car and gave her his heart-stopping smile.

'All ready? That's great! Lucy, I don't think you've met Isobel, have you?'

The other girl got out of the car gracefully and held out her hand to Lucy. 'No, we haven't, but we've spoken on the phone, I think?'

Lucy's heart had sunk at the sight of her. Soignée and sophisticated, she looked perfectly capable of handling anything that came her way.

'Have we? Oh, yes, perhaps we have...' Lucy held out a hand, not really concentrating on her words, just wondering why JJ felt he had to have a minder whenever he saw her.

'I'm afraid Isobel and I are going to have to work on our way. You don't mind, do you?' Again he smiled at her, and she shook her head. Quickly he put her case in the back, next to two others. 'I hope you won't be too cramped. This car is really only a two-seater, but it was Isobel's idea that this would be a good way to catch up on work, and it shouldn't take us too long to get there.'

'Oh, no, I'll be fine!' she assured them both, as she squeezed her long legs into the narrow space behind the two seats.

'I don't think this was such a good idea, after all!' JJ frowned as he looked at her. 'You look frightfully uncomfortable!' He bent forward across her body to try to rearrange the luggage. She held her breath as his body touched hers, but he seemed to be quite unaffected by the contact.

'No, really, I shall be quite all right...'

Blue eyes, crinkled with sudden amusement, turned to meet hers. 'If you say so. But I'll take you out for a proper dinner tonight to make up for it!'

Lucy smiled back at him. 'I'll look forward to it,' she answered demurely. He grinned as he withdrew himself.

She spent the whole journey studying the back of his neck, trying to suppress an urge to run her hands over his thick, dark hair. JJ dictated continuously, keeping his secretary fully occupied, as he drove the big car fast towards Paris, only occasionally letting his eyes meet hers in the driving mirror.

By the time they reached Paris she was strung almost to exhaustion by the sexual tension she could feel between them. Quite regardless of their silence, their bodies were still communicating with each other in a distinctly disturbing way.

The powerful car turned through the confusing streets of Paris without hesitation as he turned into the rue Faubourg St-Honoré to pull up with a flourish in front of the hotel.

'Lucy, I'm going to drop you off now before taking Isobel on to Pascale's home where she's staying tonight. You must be foully uncomfortable, so try to get a rest... There are one or two things I still have to do, but it shouldn't be too long before I'll join you.' They all got out of the car as the *baggagiste* expertly collected the luggage, and Lucy was uncomfortably stiff.

'You poor girl, I'm a brute!' JJ said as he took her arm. 'Wait in the car, Isobel, I won't be a moment.' Lucy turned to say goodbye and was taken aback by the sudden expression of fury she surprised on the other girl's face. It was smoothly wiped off, though, as she caught Lucy's expression.

'I'm sorry you've had such an uncomfortable journey,' Isobel interrupted, 'but JJ's got a lot to catch up with, particularly since Pascale let him down, so I hope you'll forgive me! He has to work so hard on these new projects that he can't really afford any time off, and JJ and I are used to working odd hours in odd places...' Her voice had dropped suggestively on the last sentence, as they faced each other alone, JJ having already walked into the hotel. 'I'm afraid business always takes priority over pleasure, but I expect you have already found that out since he has bought your fields, haven't you?'

Luckily Lucy wasn't given a chance to reply as JJ returned with a key, which he handed to her.

'I'll see you later!' His eyes promised her heaven, but he contented himself by just giving her a quick kiss on the cheek before getting back into the car.

Alone in their suite, Lucy was thoughtful as she looked down on to the large, peaceful inner courtyard. It was so quiet that it was hard to believe she was in the heart of Paris. Isobel hadn't exactly wasted much time before making her feelings clear. Vivvy was right, she had her claws into her boss and she wasn't going to let go without a fight. Her luggage had been moved into the big double room, and, knowing that had to be a mistake, she moved it towards the small single room that led off the drawing-room, which she guessed was hers.

She stripped off her clothes and walked into the adjoining bathroom. The best thing for her cramped limbs would be a hot shower. She protected her hair, then lifted her face into the warm, stinging spray, allowing the tension in her body to relax in the heat. Feeling better, she wrapped herself in one of the thick towelling bathrobes provided and went to lie on the bed. Her thoughts weren't too happy as she allowed the poison in Isobel's last words to slip in and take root in her mind, although she tried hard to reject them. He had got everything from her that he wanted, except one thing, and she knew that she was powerless to deny him that last conquest, even if it was to mean no more to him than a casual affair on his part.

She drifted into a light doze and awoke suddenly, forgetting where she was. She stretched luxuriously, then opened her eyes to see JJ standing by the door looking down at her with blazing blue eyes, the message in them impossible to mistake. He was so much the embodiment of her dreams that she smiled brilliantly at him, stretching out her arms in welcome. She thought he gave a small half-groan before coming to join her on the bed.

His hand made short work of the towelling robe, and soon she was lying naked in his arms. He had shed his jacket and tie, and his hands and mouth were sending her into a state of ecstasy bordering on delirium as he explored her body with an eagerness that matched her own. With trembling fingers she undid the buttons of his shirt, desperate to feel his skin on hers, as with a little moan she arched her body towards his.

Quickly and with an economy of effort he rid himself of the rest of his clothes as, impatient at the delay, she pulled him close to her again. The fire of their passion for each other threatened to consume them mindlessly, but he refused to let that happen. The feel of his sensitive fingers exploring her body was as erotic as she had imagined, and she began to shake in his arms, her own hands running feverishly over his smoothly muscled body. She felt a great hunger for him, as if by surrendering to his possession she could once more become herself instead of this wild, possessed creature totally at his mercy.

Later he bent over to look into her face, the blue eyes brilliant and dancing, but also possessive.

'I've never wanted any woman as much as I wanted you... And never, not even in my wildest dreams, did I think it would be as good as this!'

Gently she put up one finger to trace his mouth lovingly. 'Me, too,' she whispered. He smiled at her, playing with the long hair that lay spread out on the pillow behind her, and she felt her body tighten again with all the love she was feeling for this man, who was so capable of transporting her to paradise.

Then he murmured, 'Why did you come to my room? Was it to make me feel guilty for giving you such an uncomfortable ride this afternoon?'

'Your room? I thought it was mine!'

'I told them downstairs to give you the big room!'

She bit her lip, suddenly embarrassed. 'They did, but I thought they'd made a mistake, so I moved in here.'

He grinned. 'Don't think I'm complaining...' His finger started to trace a complicated pattern on her body. 'Do you still want to go out to dinner? Or shall I order something to be sent up here?' The warmth in his eyes made her blush, and she tried to cover her body, but his hands quickly stopped her.

'No, don't move! I like you like this...' he teased, but the passion they felt for each other was too new to have been so easily slaked, and, this time slowly, he began to make love to her again.

Later, much later, he ordered dinner for them both and kept her in a constant state of laughter with his bubbling high spirits as he teased her mercilessly, but never once did he mention love. They moved into the big bed and slept in each other's arms, and twice more in the night he woke her to be a willing partner in the game of love they had instigated. Each time he brought her to such a state of ecstatic fulfilment that she wanted to die.

Lucy had given up waiting for him to tell her he loved her, it didn't seem important as she lay in his arms. The physical pleasure they were able to give each other made it seem unimportant for the moment. He lay asleep next to her, his heartbeat now regular and slow. The thin shaft of light through the thick curtains where they did not quite meet allowed her to see that he looked much younger and slightly vulnerable, and her heart turned over with love.

Slowly and carefully, so not to disturb him, she slipped out of bed and into the bathroom to run herself a long, scented, luxurious bath. She felt intensely alive this morning and thought lazily how stupid she had been to deny them this pleasure they had in each other's bodies, but how could she have guessed it would be like this? The whole experience was so new to her, and so different from her one experiment before, when she was so much younger, that how could she have imagined that it would be so marvellous?

Quietly she slipped out of the big room and through to the smaller one where all her clothes were, and started to get dressed. She was in the bathroom, just finishing her make-up, when she heard the phone by the bed begin its discreet ring. Surprised, she picked it up.

'I'm sorry to disturb the great lover,' Isobel's voice said, 'but if you can tear yourself away you'd better come downstairs. We've got problems with the ministry, and that nice little "thank you and goodbye" bracelet you asked me to get for you in London is still in my bag! I'm in the bar, having a coffee if you want come down and collect it quickly.' The phone went dead in Lucy's hand.

She was still sitting on the bed, holding the phone, when JJ walked in.

'Good morning, my darling! Are you ordering breakfast? I'm very hungry this morning...'

With an enormous effort Lucy pulled herself together. 'No, no, that was Isobel. She's waiting for you downstairs, apparently there are problems...' He too looked vital and alive this morning. He'd had a shower and shaved, but his hair was still wet, and he was wearing only a towel twisted around his waist.

'Oh, hell! That means my morning with you has gone ... I'm sorry, sweetheart.' He came to sit next to her, and nuzzled her ear gently. 'I've got a present for you, but as it's rather special ...'

Lucy stood up swiftly. 'No! I don't want a present!' Suddenly she lost her temper and turned on him. 'Isobel's just mentioned that "thank you and goodbye" bracelet that you inconveniently left in her bag yesterday!' she told him, sarcastically. 'You can save your money this time. Keep it for the next girl who gives you what you want!'

'Hey, darling!'

'Don't "darling" me! Keep your endearments and your presents for those that want them! Oh,' she had trouble keeping her tears back, 'how could you?'

JJ looked absolutely shattered when she first started to talk then he too got angry. 'You've got a talent amounting to genius for jumping to the wrong conclusions! I don't know what's gone wrong in your twisted little mind, but it seems that love and trust are two words that don't feature largely in your vocabulary! You've obviously got some hang-up about men and sex, because it seems that you are incapable of having a normal relationship with anyone. Well, I'm not going to allow you to push your guilt for what happened last night on to me! I wouldn't have laid a finger on you unless you asked for it, and, boy, did you ask! You need a fairly long session with a psychiatrist to try and untie some of those knots, so you can live a normal life for a change. All this trying to escape back into the past isn't doing you any good at all!' he jeered.

'Still trying to tell me what to do with my life, Mr God Almighty O'Donnell? Clever you might be with your business, but you haven't got one clue about what goes on in my mind! And I'm not a neurotic mess! You're just not used to anyone not allowing you to get your own way! You can't just buy me off with a bracelet...'

'Oh, lord! You're not still harping on that? I told you, you've got the wrong end of the stick...'

She shrugged her shoulders. 'It's unimportant now, isn't it? We've got to the truth at last! You've just been trying a bit of amateur psychology on me, like all the other men I've known! Let's get her into bed and all the problems will disappear... You're not even original in your approach... Oh, hell! Why should I have thought you'd be any different from the others?' Swiftly she bent down to collect her bag and jacket that were on the chair, half blinded by tears which she angrily dashed away. 'I'm not staying here any more, I'll find somewhere else!'

He was watching her with an arrested expression on his face, as if something she had said had been important. 'You don't have to do that. I'll have your things moved into the big room, and you can have your own key. This smaller room is often let separately.'

'I don't want the big room!' she half sobbed.

'All right! Calm down, Lucy... You can keep this room if you'd rather. Look, be sensible! You can't go galloping all over Paris looking for a room, you might be late for the wedding!'

She looked at his face suspiciously.

'No strings, I promise!' His face was deadpan, with no sign of laughter or any other emotion, and she sniffed before hunting wildly in her bag for a hankie.

'All right!' she agreed, a little ungraciously.

'Now, before I leave you, order breakfast. Too much emotion on an empty stomach won't give you a good start to the day. Think what damage you'll do to my ego if you faint in church!' She gave him a wary half-smile. 'That's better! No, you needn't look worried! I shan't come near you until you've had time to think things out, then we can talk!' He collected his clothes and left the room, shutting the communicating door firmly behind him.

For the rest of the morning, even when she was changing for the wedding, Lucy's thoughts chased each other around in her head like rats in a trap. Words like 'neurotic' and 'incapable of having a normal relationship with anyone' made her blood boil, but then she remembered he thought she knew nothing of 'love and trust'... That made her ask why she had been so ready to believe ill of him.

Maybe she was lacking in trust, but it was based on fear. Fear of committing herself before she knew how he felt about her, the age-old dilemma of women everywhere in the world.

The physical attraction between them was so strong that it left little room for other, finer feelings. Her body had no such inhibitions about him, so why should she always hold part of herself back? She could find no answer to that as she changed into the dusky pink silk suit that did wonders for her tanned complexion. She rolled her hair up so that it would look neat and tidy under the small pink hat which matched her outfit, and slipped on her high-heeled navy shoes. Her sheer stockings did not hide the tan of her legs, and after a last look in the mirror she was ready to leave.

In the church she found herself sitting with Jean-Louis' family, but JJ was the other side of the church. She knew she looked good because of all the admiring eyes on her. There were some of the friends from their childhood in the church and she knew JJ would not find it easy to monopolise her afterwards because there were too many people who would want to talk to her. Anyway, she noticed sourly that he had Isobel next to him, looking smart and elegant in cream. To start with she had been surprised that Isobel should have been staying with Pascale, until she remembered that the two girls had been working together.

Pascale greeted her with sly malice as she kissed her at the reception afterwards. 'Isobel was sorry she had to worry JJ with business so early this morning!'

Lucy looked back at her with simulated surprise. 'Did she? I'm sorry, I wouldn't know, I wouldn't hear the phone in my room, anyway.'

Pascale looked a bit disconcerted for a moment, then her old confidence came back.

'It's fun being a bride, Lucy, you should try it some time!'

'I expect I will, when I'm ready!' she answered back, grateful that her attention was now to be claimed by Jean-Louis, who greeted her enthusiastically in spite of the fact that Pascale still held on to one of his arms.

'Beautiful cousin! Now I can kiss you without making my wife jealous!'

'I wouldn't depend on it!' she answered drily.

He gave Pascale a teasing smile. 'Maybe we will have to marry Lucy off to make her really happy!'

'Ah! But that's not so easy, is it, Lucy?' Pascale was so obviously enjoying her triumph that she did not have the heart to spoil her day.

'No... I shall have to come to you for advice, won't I?' she laughed, before moving on. The lunch was arranged formally, and Lucy was sitting with the family, nowhere near JJ, but she had plenty of opportunity of studying how Isobel was managing to monopolise his attention.

He caught up with her later, when all the speeches were over, and the atmosphere was more relaxed and cheerful. His eyes were warm and slightly proprietorial as they roved intimately over her body. 'You look good enough to eat in that outfit!'

She answered him with a wary smile, but she was all too aware of his dark elegance. Last night was too close in both their memories for either of them to be totally comfortable standing near each other. He gave her a smile of lazy charm that instantly had all her pulses racing.

'I suppose you noticed the bracelet on Pascale's wrist?'

'What?'

'You seemed so concerned with it this morning, and I thought she would have been certain to mention it to you!' His eyes glinted with amusement as they took in the shock in hers. 'It was a "thank you" for all the work she did in setting up my latest deal.' He closed one of his hands around her slender wrist. 'Later on this evening I'm going to come and knock on your door and ask you out to dinner. You and I are going to talk, there's a lot that needs straightening out between us.' His voice became very soft. 'Of course, you can always refuse to answer, but I've never thought you were a coward... Agreed?'

When he looked at her like that there could be no question of her refusing him anything, but she wasn't prepared to let him know just yet quite what dominion he had over her.

'I'll think about it!' she answered lightly before allowing her attention to be diverted by Jean-Louis' father, who seemed to find a great deal of pleasure in being in her company. JJ watched her being led away, but the smile was still in his eyes; he raised his glass to her in a silent toast, and she answered his smile with one of her own.

She had been given a lift by some of Jean-Louis' cousins back to the hotel, and as she was waiting to get her key from the *concierge* she was handed a message. It was from Marie, and once she read it she turned back to the desk.

'Can you get me a car and driver to take me back to my home in Normandy?'

'Certainly, *mademoiselle*. The matter is urgent?'

'Yes. I wish to leave as soon as possible.'

'There will be no problem. If you call the *baggagiste* as soon as you are packed, your luggage will be brought down immediately.' He looked into the computer screen as he spoke to her. 'Your account has already been settled by Mr O'Donnell...'

Without wasting any more time she went up to her room to change and pack, a driving urgency to be home putting everything else out of her mind.

CHAPTER NINE

WITHIN twenty minutes, thanks to the hotel's efficiency, Lucy had left, all her thoughts caught up with one small dog who had run away and then been hit by a car. Let him live, please, she prayed, her fingers tightly crossed.

It was not until they had been driving some time that she suddenly remembered JJ, and the fact that in her rush she had left no message for him.

'Oh, no!' The driver, who had so far been discreet and silent, looked a query. 'Please can you stop as soon as you see a phone?'

'Certainly, *mademoiselle*.' It didn't take him long to find one, and he was able to give her the hotel number. She was put through to the suite, and Isobel answered.

'Can I speak to JJ, please?' Lucy enquired breathlessly. 'It's Lucy.'

'He isn't available at the moment,' the cool voice replied. 'Can I give him a message?'

'Please, if you would!' Lucy answered. 'Tell him Teapot's had an accident, and I've had to rush home. Tell him also that I'm sorry I had to let him down...'

'No problem,' came back the answer, then the line went dead.

She might at least have asked how he was, Lucy thought indignantly, even if he was only a dog... She wondered what she was doing in the suite; surely they couldn't still be working? And if they were, then why hadn't she allowed her to speak to JJ? It wasn't hard to guess that jealousy was the cause, and Lucy gave a mental shrug; nothing really mattered at the moment except that her dog should not die.

Marie greeted her thankfully, almost in tears, when she arrived. 'It's going to be all right, Mademoiselle Lucy! See, there he is lying by the cooker, the rogue.'

Lucy walked quickly over to him and bent over to touch him gently. Sleepily he opened one eye, and gave a faint wag. There was a cut on his head, which had been stitched. It looked ugly, and he smelt faintly still of the anaesthetic the vet had used.

'He has been very lucky!' Marie told her severely. 'No bones broken, just bruising, and that cut on the head... But when I first found him! *Oh, la la,* I thought he was dead... The blood!' She threw up her hands.

'I'm sorry, you've had a beastly time with him, I can see. But, oh, Marie! I'm so pleased he's going to be all right...' She sat down quickly at the table.

It had cost her a horrifying amount of money to get home, but she thought it was worth it for her peace of mind. Teapot was better left where he was, to sleep off the effects of his accident, while she and Marie ate a scrap dinner near him. She thought it unlikely that he would stir in the night, and now her thoughts were free again to follow their own inclinations.

She hoped JJ would forgive her for dashing off, and thought he was fond enough of the little dog to understand why she should have left so precipitately. Anyway, he was due back at the farm tomorrow, so their talk would only have to be postponed twenty-four hours. It seemed she had been misjudging him, if his tone and looks were anything to go by, and she couldn't help feeling excited at the thought of their meeting tomorrow. She could even laugh foolishly at herself for supposing the bracelet had been intended for her. She had certainly over-reacted this morning...

This morning! It was hard to believe that it had only been such a short while since she had been in his arms. Their one night together had felt so right, so perfect, that in retrospect she wondered even more why she had been so silly. She supposed, if she was to be honest with herself, that she had been frightened to admit that she owed her future happiness to a man who had the power to send her spinning crazily to the stars. Perhaps that had

always been the real problem between them. She
had refused to recognise the primitive emotion that
had driven them both almost to madness.

She knew, she had always known, that it was
wrong to base a marriage on those feelings only,
there had to be more, and on her part there was.
She loved many things about him: his quick mind,
his kindness, his seeming understanding of her
feelings. She could have sworn that he was not a
man who was interested in casual sex, that he was
fastidious in his pleasure. The thought warmed her.
Although he had never outwardly spoken of love,
surely she had felt it as he held her close in the
night?

She woke early the next morning and, on
checking that her small dog was as right as could
be expected, began to plan her day. She had to take
him into the vet's again to be fitted with a wide
plastic collar to stop him scratching the stitches in
his head, then the day was her own. Teapot was
obviously stiff and uncomfortable, and her heart
bled for him as she watched him hobble out into
the yard. Luckily he still had pills to be taken, which
would mitigate his pain for the next two days or
so, but even so she suffered for him.

There would be no point in going over to Grande
Ferme until the evening, JJ would be far too busy
to spare her any time earlier in the day, but the
hours dragged until it was time for her to change.

It had been a hot day, and the air still shimmered with heat, so she chose to wear only shorts and a low-cut, thin white cotton shirt. She had no need to be formal with him now, and she knew he liked to see her long legs.

Teapot was dozing as she left, and she slipped out quietly, determined not to disturb him. She could hear some machines still working as she walked over the farm, marvelling at how much had been accomplished in such a short time. There was almost a proprietorial interest as she stopped often to study everything that was being done. For the first time she began to identify JJ's interests as her own, and she thought that, once she had got used to the idea, it would be fun to help him.

One of his first jobs had been converting the old farm buildings into homes for the resident staff. They were attractively based round the old courtyard, and already it was hard to believe that so short a time ago they had been home to generations of cows. There were few signs left that it had ever been a working farm, so quickly had the changes taken place.

JJ was sitting alone on the terrace drinking some wine when she first saw him. Unable to help herself, she broke into a run.

'Hi!' she said, breathlessly. 'Sorry about last night, but he's going to be all right!'

She got a shock when, rather shyly, she allowed her eyes to meet his. Cold and hard, they studied her aloofly, rather as they had when they had first met. There was no warmth in his voice either as he asked, 'What are you doing here?'

She was totally taken aback and bewildered. 'I, well, I... I thought you'd like to know that...' She faltered to a stop.

'You thought I'd still be interested to find out why you ran out on me last night?' he queried sarcastically.

'No! I mean, you know why...'

'Yes, I do, don't I?' he riposted savagely. 'Although why you think that gives you the right to walk in on me now I can't imagine!'

'JJ?' she pleaded. 'I thought you would understand?'

'Did you? Well, you're wrong! Our pleasant little interlude is over! I'm too busy to waste any more time on you...' he told her cruelly. 'The sooner I get this project finished, then the quicker I can leave!' He turned away from her to pour himself another glass of wine. 'Forgive me for not asking you to join me...' Shattered, she too turned away so he wouldn't see the betraying tears in her eyes, as she started to make her way home, her head still held proudly until she was out of his sight.

*   *   *

Two months later Lucy held a smart gilt-edged invitation in her hand. It had come by that morning's post, and she held it carefully, wondering at the almost perfect timing of its arrival as far as she was concerned. It seemed JJ was giving a private, pre-opening party at Grande Ferme before the official opening in three weeks' time, and all their neighbours were to be invited to see for themselves the changes he had made. She had not set eyes on him since their last disastrous meeting, but, whatever her feelings, she now had a compelling reason to meet him again as soon as possible.

She had too much pride to ask for an interview, which she guessed would be turned down, but this way she would surely be able to make an opportunity to tell him what he had to know. At first she had put her missed period down to the misery she was feeling, but after she missed again for the second time she was convinced she was pregnant.

She had been careful to make sure that no one should guess her secret, not even her parents, who had just left after staying with her for two weeks. Luckily she was suffering none of the symptoms of morning sickness, and the anguish in her mind did not show. Her first immediate reaction had been one of sheer panic, but that passed. She would never be able to give her child its father, but at least she earned enough money to be able to look after herself and her baby properly.

The child would be her one link with past happiness; she had made a terrible mistake in trusting a man with her love, but that was no reason why her unborn child should suffer.

Because she was also innately honest, she knew it would be wrong to deny JJ the knowledge that he had fathered her child. She would make it clear that she expected nothing from him; indeed, the thought that he might feel obliged to contribute towards her expenses made her feel ill. She pulled herself together with the idea that it was most likely that he would repudiate any responsibility. Although that hurt, it would probably be the easiest way out.

She had thought long and hard about why he should have treated her so cruelly, but had been unable to come up with an answer. She had always considered him a kind man, and it had been difficult to come to terms with the fact that she had been right to have reservations about him. She did feel bitter that she had allowed her body to betray her, but she knew that she had no one to blame but herself for the mess she had got into.

Teapot had been her great comfort and solace, and if to start with she had cried herself to sleep, he had done his best to console her. He had become even more her inseparable companion, and they had spent long, lazy days on the beach when she hadn't been working. He still proved to be a great source of inspiration, so she was able to lose herself in her work.

She wasn't altogether surprised when Jean-Louis and Pascale invited themselves to stay for the party, but she was made supremely uncomfortable when Jean-Louis told her with pride that Pascale was having a baby. It made her own position unhappier when she saw with her own eyes how carefully Jean-Louis treated his pretty young wife.

As she changed in her room she felt lonelier than she had ever felt in her life. Her misery was such that if she was given a chance to escape this self-inflicted ordeal, then she would take it, and not bother about the consequences, but it was already too late. Her only armour to hide her bruised heart was her pride and her determination to look as beautiful as a fabulous dress could make her.

It had been a crazy impulse that had made her squander her money on an *haute couture* dress that in a few months she wouldn't be able to wear, but when she put it on she knew her instinct had been right. The deceptive simplicity of the white satin made her look impossibly fragile, yet the warmth of her tanned skin gave it an erotic contrast which was irresistible. Her hair, bleached even fairer by the sun, she left to hang loose, caught only on one side by a single white rosebud in a diamond clip. She wore no other jewellery, knowing her smooth skin needed no ornament. The beautiful dress armoured her with confidence, and she had only to look at Pascale's face when they met to know that she had succeeded beyond her wildest dreams. The sulky expression on her face said it all; it was left to Jean-Louis to express his admiration.

She had already insisted on taking two separate cars, because she intended to leave early, and as she watched them drive off ahead of her she deliberately waited so she would be able to make her entrance alone. She wanted no one with her when she dropped her bombshell on JJ. She had thought it unlikely that he would come near her after their initial greeting, so she would have to make the most of her only opportunity.

She had timed her arrival to be late, so most of the guests would already be there, but not too late so that JJ would have left his position as host. Deliberately she schooled her features into serene unconcern before she entered the room where he would be waiting for her.

She heard his sudden indrawn breath as he caught sight of her. Coolly she nodded to him, ignoring his outstretched hands, and checked that they were alone. She found she couldn't quite bring herself to meet his eyes; the torment of being near to him was almost more than she could bear.

'Lucy!' He breathed her name, and she heard the raw longing behind the softly spoken word. It gave her a queer kind of pain in her heart, yet it also hardened her determination.

'I have something to tell you!' She allowed her eyes to meet his, but ignored the blazing passion she saw in them. 'It will make no difference to the way things are,' she continued with a cool smile, 'but, as you are indirectly concerned, it is right that you should know. I think I am going to have a baby, and you are the father.' Again she heard him sharply draw in his breath. 'I expect nothing from you, and want nothing from you!' The pain in her heart was now so fierce that she could hardly breathe. She drew a quivering breath, then turned away before he could see the emotion in her face.

'Lucy!' She heard the agonised protest but ignored it, moving gracefully away to mingle with his guests, intent on putting as much distance between them as possible before leaving.

'My dear girl! You look quite ravishing!' Blindly Lucy turned to face the smiling face of Vivvy. The blue eyes, so similar to her brother's, made her pull herself together. 'Tom! Tom! Come here, darling, I want you to meet Lucy.' A tall, blond man detached himself from a small group of people and came over to them, his laughing eyes appreciating every inch of Lucy's figure.

'Well, well, well! So now I understand why your brother's spent the summer out here!'

Lucy blushed under his discerning look.

'Really, darling! Where are your manners? Lucy, meet my husband, and, little though he must have recommended himself to you, he's really quite nice!' Lucy smiled at him, and gave him her hand, but inwardly she was all too aware that JJ had followed her over and was standing behind her. She could feel the goose-pimples begin to come up on her skin, but didn't know how to get away without offending Vivvy and her husband.

Tom came to her rescue. 'Go away, JJ! I want the chance to get to know this gorgeous girl without you hanging around my neck!' Without waiting to ask Lucy's permission, he swept her outside on to the terrace where a marquee had been erected and a floor put down for dancing.

'I hope you'll forgive my bad manners?' He laughed down at her face as he pulled her on to the dance-floor. 'But I'm not surprised that my devious brother-in-law has been keeping you quiet!'

She managed to answer his questions coherently, but half her mind was aware of JJ, who had accompanied his sister on to the dance-floor. It seemed as if he intended to keep a close eye on her, instead of ignoring her as she had half hoped he would.

The tumult of her emotions made it necessary that she should escape as soon as possible. She'd been stupid to think she could bear to be in the same room as JJ; the old magic of his presence was working as strongly as ever as far as she was concerned. She waited until she saw he had been caught by the local mayor. She knew from old that the mayor loved the sound of his own voice and had a strong sense of his own importance. JJ would find it difficult to escape from his clutches for some time.

She smiled up into Tom's face. 'Will you forgive me for a moment? I've just remembered I've left my bag in my car.' Lucy had done that deliberately to give her a legitimate reason for leaving Grande Ferme.

'Yes, pretty lady! But I hope we will meet again soon. Vivvy's right for once! You'll be a great addition to the family...' Just for a moment her eyes caught his, the pain in hers bringing the beginnings of a frown to his face. 'I'm sorry, Lucy, that was unforgivable of me...'

With a tremendous effort she managed to give him another smile. 'Forget it! I'm very pleased to have met you—Vivvy has talked a lot about you and your boys...'

He followed her lead. 'She's a great talker, that wife of mine! But she can also be a good listener as well.'

'I'm sure she can!' Lucy smiled politely at him. 'Now, if you will forgive me?' He let her leave reluctantly, but his eyes were slightly puzzled as he watched her walk out into the warm darkness of the night.

She had left her car in an easy position for a quick getaway, and she wasted no time in making her escape. Standing again in the kitchen of Cherrytree made her feel rather like Cinderella. Soon she would have to put her beautiful dress away, because she didn't think she would ever wear it again, and she looked sadly at its gleaming white beauty. It had had only a tiny moment of glory, but long enough for her purposes. Marie was out, so she and Teapot were alone.

Tomorrow, after Jean-Louis and Pascale had returned to Paris, she was going to have to replan her life. She wanted her baby to be born in her own country, and that was going to be complicated, because of Teapot. It would mean giving up Cherrytree Farm and going back to live in England, and the little dog would have to go into quarantine. It would also mean telling her parents what had happened, and that would not be an easy task. Feeling tired, she sat down and decided to get something to eat.

She got a horrid shock when JJ walked into the kitchen.

'What are you doing here?' She tried to grab a wildly excited small dog, but he was like a small eel and wriggled away from her to give JJ an ecstatic welcome. There was a rueful smile on JJ's face as he accepted Teapot's welcome, and noticed

her frozen expression. 'Get out! I don't want you
here... Anyway, what about your guests?'

'Vivvy has already explained that I've been suddenly called away, but I agree it would be politer
if I returned. Why don't we return together? I'm
going to announce our engagement tonight!'

Justifiably incensed, she answered, 'Oh, no,
you're not! How dare you think you can walk in
here and just take control? I haven't forgotten our
last meeting, if you have! You made it quite clear
then that you wanted nothing more to do with me!'

'I made a terrible mistake that day. I heard this
evening about Teapot being run over... Can't you
understand that I was mad with jealousy that day?
I thought you had decided to walk out on me... I
never got your message about him, you see...' He
stood up and gave her his heartwarming smile. 'I
love you, Lucy! And if I hadn't been an obstinate
fool I would have told you months ago... When I
first saw you tonight I knew that I would have to
tell you how I felt. Then you told me your news,
about the baby. Well, that really knocked me
sideways! Don't you see? We have to get married
now!'

Lucy was angrier with him than she had ever been
before. 'You are still the most arrogant man I've
ever had the misfortune to meet! You walk in here
tonight and expect me to believe that you love me
and want to marry me? Well, let me tell you, Mr

Mills ❀ Boon
WINTER
COMPETITION

How would you like a
year's supply of Mills & Boon Romances ABSOLUTELY FREE?
Well, you can win them! All you have to do is complete the word
puzzle below and send it into us by 30th June 1989.
The first five correct entries picked out of the bag after that date
will each win a year's supply of Mills & Boon Romances (Ten
books every month - **worth over £100!**) What could be easier?

```
C W A E T A N R E B I H
H R I C E R W O L G M Y
I F R O S T A O E L U Y
L N I B O R U D R I V Y
L B L E A K B W I I N F
T O G L O V E S E A R R
S O S G O L R W I E T E
T T C H F I R E L R O E
S K A T E M Y C I K S Z
I Y R R E M I P I N E E
N A F D E C E M B E R N
N C E M I S T L E T O E
```

~~Ivy~~
Frost
~~Bleak~~
~~Boot~~
~~Robin~~
~~Yule~~
~~Freeze~~

~~Radiate~~
~~Chill~~
~~Glow~~
~~Ice~~
Hibernate
~~Icicle~~
~~Gloves~~

~~December~~
Skate
Mistletoe
~~Fire~~
~~Log~~
~~Scarf~~
Berry

~~Star~~
~~Ski~~
~~Fan~~

~~Merry~~
~~Pine~~

**PLEASE TURN
OVER FOR
DETAILS
ON HOW
TO ENTER**

How to enter

All the words listed overleaf, below the word puzzle, are hidden in the grid. You can find them by reading the letters forwards, backwards, up or down, or diagonally. When you find a word, circle it, or put a line through it. After you have found all the words the remaining letters (which you can read from left to right, from the top of the puzzle through to the bottom) will spell a secret message.

Don't forget to fill in your name and address in the space provided and pop this page in an envelope (you don't need a stamp) and post it today. Hurry - competition ends 30th June 1989

Only one entry per household please.

Mills & Boon Competition,
FREEPOST,
P.O. Box 236,
Croydon,
Surrey CR9 9EL.

Secret message _Warm your winter with Romance._

Name. _Sonia Munro_

Address _Dalreoch, lower Dunain, Inverness, Scotland,_

Postcode _IV3 6JX_

COMP5